M000207790
MgRonald.
MgRonald. Hamburger
BEEF 100%
真奥
team
MgRonald

Emi Yusa
&Chiho Sasaki

THE DEVIL IS A PART-TIMER!
8
SATOSHI WAGAHARA
ILLUSTRATION BY
029 (ONIKU)

CONTENTS!

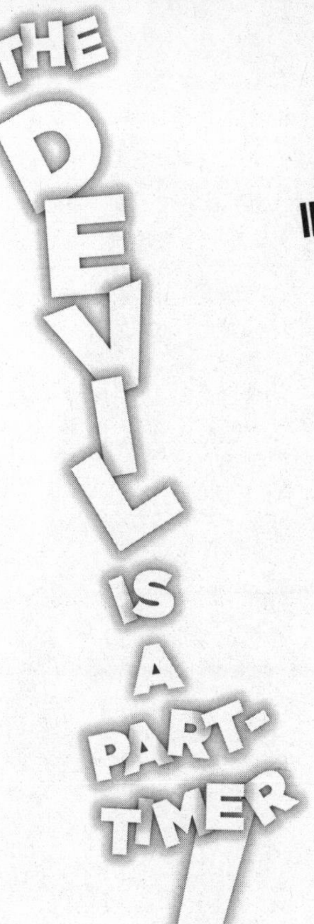

8

SATOSHI WAGAHARA

ILLUSTRATED BY 029 (ONIKU)

NEW YORK

THE DEVIL IS A PART-TIMER!, Volume 8
SATOSHI WAGAHARA, ILLUSTRATION BY 029 (ONIKU)

Translation by Kevin Gifford
Cover art by 029 (oniku)

This book is a work of fiction. Names, characters, places, and incidents are the product of the author's imagination or are used fictitiously. Any resemblance to actual events, locales, or persons, living or dead, is coincidental.

Edited by ASCII MEDIA WORKS
First published in 2013 by KADOKAWA CORPORATION, Tokyo.

English translation rights arranged with KADOKAWA CORPORATION, Tokyo, through Tuttle-Mori Agency, Inc., Tokyo.

Yen On
1290 Avenue of the Americas
New York, NY 10104

Visit us at yenpress.com
facebook.com/yenpress
twitter.com/yenpress
yenpress.tumblr.com
instagram.com/yenpress

First Yen On Edition: August 2017

Yen On is an imprint of Yen Press, LLC.
The Yen On name and logo are trademarks of Yen Press, LLC.

The publisher is not responsible for websites (or their content) that are not owned by the publisher.

Library of Congress Cataloging-in-Publication Data
Names: Wagahara, Satoshi. | 029 (Light novel illustrator) illustrator. | Gifford, Kevin, translator.
Title: The devil is a part-timer! / Satoshi Wagahara ; illustration by 029 (oniku) ; translation by Kevin Gifford.
Other titles: Hataraku Maousama!. English
Description: First Yen On edition. | New York, NY : Yen On, 2015–
Identifiers: LCCN 2015028390 |
ISBN 9780316383127 (v. 1 : pbk.) |
ISBN 9780316385015 (v. 2 : pbk.) |
ISBN 9780316385022 (v. 3 : pbk.) |
ISBN 9780316385039 (v. 4 : pbk.) |
ISBN 9780316385046 (v. 5 : pbk.) |
ISBN 9780316385060 (v. 6 : pbk.) |
ISBN 9780316469364 (v. 7 : pbk.) |
ISBN 9780316473910 (v. 8 : pbk.)
Subjects: | CYAC: Fantasy.
Classification: LCC PZ7.1.W34 Ha 2015 | DDC [Fic]—dc23
LC record available at http://lccn.loc.gov/2015028390

ISBNs: 978-0-316-47391-0 (paperback)
978-0-316-47417-7 (ebook)

3 5 7 9 10 8 6 4 2

LSC-C

Printed in the United States of America

PROLOGUE

She never thought this day would come. Even now, she found herself at a crossroads.

Taking an impartial look at her position, this was a clear dereliction of duty. A breach of trust, even. Although, if you put it that way, she had been abandoning her sworn duty from the very start—ever since that single moment—and just aimlessly passing the days ever since.

If she wanted to try, she could come up with any number of excuses for it. But if asked whether she was taking any kind of active approach to the issues in her life, the answer was a resolute no. She was merely going with the flow. Her back was turned to her mission; she was too focused on tidying up the problems that loomed in front of her face—and before she knew it, it had grown comfortable to her. Now, her initial mission was starting to seem not so important any longer.

It was time to come out with it. By now…

"I'm not sure I know whether it's really okay to kill the Devil King any longer."

"…Oh reeeally now?"

There was not a shred of reproach to her old friend's voice on the other end of the line. If anything, it had a sense of relief to it, albeit one still tempered with concern.

"I kind of had a feeeeling it would wind up like this."

"Wind up like what?"

Her friend chuckled. *"Like, by the time we meet again, you still wouldn't have slain the Devvvvil King or annnything."*

"Yeah, no defense there, I guess."

"Oh, it's all riiiight! If that's the way you feeeel, Emilia, there must be some good reeeason for it. Besides..." The friend's voice took on a more serious, practiced tone. It was rare, coming from her. *"You've got every right to choose, Emilia."*

"Choose what?" came the befuddled reply.

"When Olba betraaayed you, Emilia, you could have easily exacted your reveeenge against all of us."

"Revenge? Oh, come on, why would I do that to—"

"I'm not talking about meee or Albert, now! I mean the Churrrch, or Ente Isla as a whole, you knoooow? The entire world turned its back on you. If you decided to get vengeance, nobody had any right to stop you...even if they waaanted to."

"Oh, that's what you mean?"

If she were a young Hero, thoughts truly filled with nothing but murder for the Devil King, the idea of her friends betraying her and the world reacting to news of her death with idle complacence would have filled her with deep despair. But these days, it didn't.

"Look, I live in a world where everyone's got cell phones and the Internet's everywhere you go, but it's still hard to get info you can rely on. I'm not gonna lose any sleep if a world like Ente Isla gets the wrong idea like that. It's still a feudal society."

"Interrr...what?"

"Never mind. Besides, I'm too much of a simpleminded ditz for stupid stuff like that to even occur to me."

"Well, I dunno what you meeean, but all riiight. If you ever do start to get feelings along those lines, be sure to let me know, okaaay?"

"Are you trying to tempt me or something?" she said with a laugh. "You want me to do that, or not?"

"Oh," came the quick reply. *"Whatever path you choose, Emilia, I'm still on your siiide, all right? I'm not at all against destroying the worrrld, even."*

"The strongest Church conjurer in the world really shouldn't make idle threats like that. Don't blame me if the Church starts keeping their eyes on you."

"They've already got their eyes on me so much! I'm about ready to pluck them out and sellll them as marbles to the local kids."

The girl looked at her feet, not too sure how serious her friend was being. Near them was a backpack, filled to the brim with an assortment of bric-a-brac.

"Well, see you this weekend."

"Absoluuutely!" chirped Emeralda Etuva, the most powerful sorceress in Ente Isla.

THE HERO DEMANDS A LITTLE TIME OFF

Time passed, calmly and breezily, just like it always did around the dinner table. All the usual sights were there—the freshly cooked rice, aromatic steam rising above it, and the miso soup with chopped carrots in it. Thanks to a fancy new microwave-safe cooking sheet, grilled fish had become a regular presence on the menu. The cold tofu that served as a side dish was festooned with shredded ginger, and at the center of the table, a bubbling bowl of *shigiyaki* (soup made from eggplant, miso sauce, and sesame seeds) grabbed the most attention.

The news program on the TV was covering some regional festival or another as its top story, indicating wordlessly that nothing disturbing or otherwise newsworthy had taken place today to disrupt the serenity. The window, open wide, let just the suggestion of a breeze through in the late afternoon, bringing hints of the city bustle surrounding the room inside.

To everyone in the tiny apartment in an even tinier corner of Tokyo, everything about this dinner suggested everything was truly well with the world. And all it took to destroy this atmosphere, this bubble of good cheer that surrounded Room 201 of the Villa Rosa Sasazuka apartment building in Shibuya ward, was a single sentence.

"I'm going back home for a little while."

The words, by themselves, seemed innocent enough. But in the context of this apartment, they were a bomb disguised as a herald of peace. Everyone froze.

"Huh?"

"What?"

"Buh?"

"Wh-what on earth are you saying?!"

"Y-your home?!"

"I like tofu!"

Six different people gave six very different reactions to the girl who lit the fuse—Emi Yusa, better known as Emilia Justina, the Hero of her home world of Ente Isla. She blinked.

"Wh...what's with *that* reaction?"

The Devil King of this castle—aka Sadao Maou—had been seated at the apartment's computer desk, textbook in one hand. His face stiffened.

"I think we're having a little trouble parsing what that's supposed to mean," he supplied.

"What?" Emi replied, puzzled.

"Emilia," came a voice from inside the second level of the closet—from the person who usually would've been seated in front of the laptop. "You mind rephrasing that a little? 'Cause I think Chiho Sasaki's going into a panic, imagining you, Maou, and Alas Ramus living in some white-picket-fence dream house..."

"Urushihara!!"

"Agh! Whoa, look out—"

Hanzou Urushihara, better known as the fallen angel Lucifer, grinned. He was the collective baggage of Devil's Castle, and perhaps the second most appropriate thing in the world to store in a closet. Chiho Sasaki, the red-faced high school student he'd just namechecked, responded by pushing him fully back into the closet and slamming the door.

"Whoa! Dude!" came a muffled attempt at self-defense beyond the door. "What the hell, Chiho Sasaki!!"

"That's your fault for saying all that weird stuff!" she replied as she strained to keep the door in place, face still red as she attempted to keep Urushihara where he belonged.

"Chi-Sis, you're all red!" a deviously innocent voice said at her feet. Alas Ramus, the adoptive daughter of Maou and Emi (though, really, *she* had adopted *them* more than anything) had been playing with Chiho a moment ago. Now she was stamping on a big, plastic sheet meant for teaching the alphabet.

"Oh! Hey, Alas Ramus, it's almost time for dinner, all right?" Chiho shouted in a failed attempt to change the subject. "It's time to clean up!"

"Okeh! Time to kleenup!"

The sheet was one of the fancier ones at the shop, made of sturdy enough plastic that it wouldn't tear no matter how badly it was wadded up.

"But…really, though, Yusa, what do you mean?"

Chiho dared the question as Maou watched Alas Ramus take the sheet he had spent a chunk of his earnings on and mangle it into a folded, spindled disaster.

"I, um, I meant pretty much what I said. I was just thinking I'd head back home pretty soon…"

"Wait, Emilia. What do you mean by 'home,' exactly?" came the pained question from a girl in Japanese dress, washing the utensils she had used to cook the upcoming meal.

"Well, you know… My home. On the Western Island. I grew up in a farming village called Sloane, on the far end of Saint Aile. It got razed by an army led by that freak in your closet." Emi turned a sharp eye toward the closet door. "So I was hoping I could count on you to watch these guys for me while I'm gone, Bell…"

She was talking to Crestia Bell, a powerful Ente Isla cleric who went by the name Suzuno Kamazuki while in Japan.

"Can you provide more detail, please?" the cleric inquired, rinsing the dish detergent off her hands. "I fail to understand your intentions."

"Y-yeah, Yusa! It can't be that easy to go back home, can it?"

"Oh. Yeah, sorry if I was too point-blank with that," Emi replied, chuckling at herself as she realized her mistake. "So it's like—"

Then she stopped, noticing a man standing behind Chiho and Suzuno.

"I hardly care a bit where you decide to take yourself...but I refuse to let the miso soup I slaved over go cold for *your* sake."

The voice boomed as the man held a large soup bowl in his hands. Shirou Ashiya, aka the Great Demon General Alciel, turned toward his master at the computer desk. "Your Demonic Highness, we are ready to eat. Please save your studies for later and take your seat."

"Yeah, yeah. Emi just destroyed my focus anyway."

"Hey! You mind not blaming other people for your stupidity?"

"Tofu! Al-cell! Tofu!"

Somewhere along the line, Alas Ramus had approached the legs of the miso-toting Ashiya.

"Now, now," Suzuno said as he grabbed her away. "It's dangerous to scare someone carrying a big bowl like that. Back to Mommy with you!"

Alas Ramus walked up to Emi, still not entirely convinced of the logic of this.

"Mommy! Tofu!"

"All right. Once we all sit down at the table, okay? Don't put any ginger on my cold tofu, Alciel. I'm gonna give some of it to Alas Ramus."

The family had made a regular habit out of giving a morsel of either Emi's or Maou's meal to Alas Ramus. But, after carefully studying Alas Ramus and Emi's portion of tofu, Ashiya shook his head.

"I refuse. What will you do if Alas Ramus turns into a picky eater?"

It was such a strange conversation for a Hero to have with a Great Demon General that no one could even begin to figure out what went wrong between the two of them.

"Ooh," interjected the only native Japanese citizen in the room. "Ashiya, I don't think ginger is too good to feed to a baby..."

"It is vital that she get used to the taste of pungent vegetables," Ashiya countered—a rarity, considering how weak he usually was to Chiho's lectures. "The sooner she learns to enjoy this taste, the more exciting every meal will be for her..."

"Oh, but I get where she's coming from. I kinda got issues with ginger, too—"

"And you call yourself a fallen angel, Lucifer?!" Ashiya fumed.

"Dude, what do you want from me? I lived all this time without ever having ginger before. Did, like, ginger ever show up in the mythology about me?"

He had a point. Neither in the lofty heavens, nor beneath the brightest flaming pyre of the demon realms, did there exist neat little squares of tofu with shredded ginger on top. That was enough for Urushihara's argument to gain an ally for a change.

"I'm, uh, not too good with it, either..."

The pathetic-sounding statement, uttered as he settled down at the table, came from the great Devil King Satan himself, the monster that unified the demon realms and had been just a breath away from adding the human world of Ente Isla to his list of glorious conquests. And yet here, inside this tiny apartment, mankind finally discovered the one weak point of their future nemesis: The Devil King did not like ginger on top of chilled tofu.

"Maou..."

"My liege..."

"Devil King, of all the simpering things to say..."

Maou withered under the half-pained, half-pitying expressions that Chiho, Ashiya, and Suzuno put forth before him.

"L-look, I can eat it, okay? Have I ever not earned my clean-plate award?"

"Let's just have Daddy eat Alas Ramus's ginger then, okay?" said the Hero Emilia, unfailingly striking at the Devil King's soft, unguarded underbelly. Soon, the operation was under way. As Chiho, Ashiya, and Suzuno looked on at the squirming Maou, Emi carefully used her chopsticks to transfer the ginger flakes over to the devil's tofu.

"Agh! Emi!" he shouted at the sight of his tofu suffering under an avalanche of ginger. Emi ignored him.

"If you don't like it," she said, "bitch at Alciel. It's not a matter of being finicky—if you feed ginger to someone Alas Ramus's age, she's gonna hate it forever. And why wouldn't she, if even the Devil King aiming to take over the world doesn't like it?"

"Oof..."

Maou couldn't find anything to counter with. Ashiya looked equally pained. "Ngh," he groaned. "Bell, surely you have something to say about this!"

"And surely, Alciel, you see how cruel ginger would be to a tender child such as this... Emilia, I have some low-salt soy sauce in my room. Let me go fetch it. It should be better for Alas Ramus."

Suzuno padded off to Room 202 next door. Urushihara looked on as he extended his chopsticks over to the eggplant stew in the center of the table. "Man," he muttered, "I worry about Alas Ramus's future if everyone's gonna spoil her like this..."

"Urushihara! We have to say thanks for the meal first! Alas Ramus is here and everything!"

"Eesh. I had no idea raising a kid was so hard. I wouldn't want *that* to happen to her..."

"Dude, Maou, why're you looking at me when you say that?"

"Why don't you ask yourself that?" the merciless Chiho shot back. "Alas Ramus is a lot more sensible and well-mannered than you are."

"Right. Here's the soy sauce."

Ashiya, his original topic of conversation now thoroughly in the past, resigned himself to surrender as Suzuno returned with her sauce bottle.

"...So be it. Let's eat before the miso soup's at room temperature."

"Hey, lemme get some more rice, Ashiya."

"Oh, wait! My mom gave me some boneless fried chicken to share," the flustered Chiho said as she removed a plastic container from her bag. "Can I use the oven a sec, Ashiya?"

"Ah, thank you as always, Ms. Sasaki. You will need to turn the center knob to—"

“Oh, I know. Boy, I almost completely forgot, too…”

It was a surreal sight, no doubt—the Great Demon General and Church cleric standing in the Devil’s Castle kitchen, a teenage girl bringing them some chicken, the Hero and Devil King discussing modern parenting while keeping a watchful eye on the ill-mannered fallen angel—but the way it all worked, somehow, indicated to everyone that Room 201 in Villa Rosa Sasazuka was, as always, a paragon of peace. It’d take a lot more than some trip back home to rock this boat.

Whether that was a good thing or not, none of them could say quite yet.

⁂

Right around the end of summer, a shadow clearly began to cast itself over the constantly feuding, yet oddly peaceful relationship between the Devil King and the Hero.

In the other world, after Maou tasted defeat at the hands of Emi, the resulting power vacuum had been filled by the Malebranche tribe led by Barbariccia, aiming to build a new Devil King’s Army in order to stage another Ente Isla invasion. They were buoyed by Olba Meiyer, a powerful Church official and former ally of the Hero, now hell-bent on destroying both her and the Devil King. Olba sent Farfarello, one of the Malebranche’s top generals, to Earth in order to convince Maou and Ashiya to lead their so-called New Devil King’s Army. Both Emi and Suzuno feared the worst at this wicked invitation, but despite all the catastrophes they predicted, both Maou and Ashiya refused the offer.

They could have easily sent Farfarello back to the demon realms, as they did with Ciriatto back in Choshi, or have Emi shred him to bits for them. But the boy accompanying Farfarello made matters complicated. It was Erone, a child borne from the Sephirah known as Gevurah—one of the fruits of the tree of Sephirot, the fabled Tree of Life that grew in the minds of all Church followers in Ente Isla.

Erone was similar to Alas Ramus, who was born from the Yesod

Sephirah and fused with Emi's holy sword. This occasionally gave her powers that far outclassed even the Hero and Devil King.

It remained unclear why a Sephirah child was working for one of the leaders of the Malebranche—and while Farfarello was one thing, it would be rash to do anything ill-advised to this boy. It could create new enemies for Maou and the others not just among the Malebranche, but among the heavens as well.

And even worse, Farfarello and Erone—people who had to be dealt with delicately, if at all—found out that Chiho was someone important to both Maou and Emi. If this kept up, the Malebranche—once they realized that there was no cajoling Maou or Ashiya to join their horde—might decide to take her hostage to force their hand.

Chiho, of course, had just as much care in her heart for Emi and Suzuno. Enough so, in fact, that she convinced them to teach her the telepathy-like Idea Link magic, so that she could send them an SOS whenever danger approached. Maou, for his part, realized there were limits to his haphazard approach to ensuring Chiho's safety. To put a final stop to the threat, he borrowed Emi's and Suzuno's powers to transform himself into the Devil King Satan—a process he made sure Farfarello bore full witness to. That was enough to indicate that all three girls played vital roles in his global conquest—and naming all of them as Great Demon Generals was enough to make Farfarello and Erone return to the demon realms without a fight. Being named as Demon Generals in front of the Malebranche enraged Emi and Suzuno, of course, but you can't make an omelet without breaking a few eggs.

This entire effort might have saved Chiho from any immediate threat from Farfarello or his tribe, but if time passed and things changed on the Ente Isla side, there was no telling what kind of presence this Chiho Sasaki, the new Satan-endorsed Great Demon General, would have in the minds of the people. It was certainly no permanent solution to Maou and Emi's problems.

So there it was, all laid out: the Malebranche attempting to rebuild Maou's army; the new child of a Sephirah; the continued mystery of what went on in the heavens. They could all feel the ill winds of another world brush against their faces—but, in the end, they had to work today if they wanted to eat tomorrow. That was how they all greeted September, a still-all-too-warm end to the summer.

⁂

Even with sunset coming just a smidge quicker than before, the sky was still ever-so-bright past seven PM, more than lively enough to light the way along the path to Sasazuka Station along the Keio Line. Emi was walking along that path with Suzuno, holding the full and satisfied Alas Ramus as she nodded off. Chiho and Maou were behind them.

Whenever Emi and Alas Ramus paid a custodial visit to Devil's Castle, Maou made every possible effort to ensure Chiho joined in on dinner. Chiho gave the reason to everyone herself: "If I'm not here, you two will just start fighting, won't you?"

With Farfarello's chaos still fresh in their minds, Maou and Emi were now trying even harder to keep things harmonious with Chiho—even if it meant her pushing them around a little. Chiho might not have known about it, but they had inadvertently heard from Chiho herself what she thought about Maou and the gang. It was so pure, so straightforward, that there was no resisting it.

But even without such weighty issues forcing their hands, having Chiho for dinner made Alas Ramus happy and ensured everyone got something decent to eat. As if to repay her, an unspoken rule was established somewhere along the line that Maou and Suzuno would walk Chiho back home for her. It was the least they could do.

"So, Emilia," Suzuno asked along the way, "what did you mean by 'returning home'?"

That line of conversation had fallen by the wayside over dinner.

"Oh! Hey, yeah!" Chiho interjected as she chatted with Maou about their jobs. "What did you mean, Yusa?"

"Oh…"

Three women walking alongside each other down a narrow side road meant that Maou had no way of inserting himself into the conversation. He trudged along, gauging the three of them as they sauntered shoulder to shoulder.

Emi looked at both of the girls' curious eyes and exhaled a little sigh.

"I'm just sick of waiting any longer."

"How so?"

"…Ever since I found the Devil King here in Japan, I've had to deal with all this trouble I never expected. And I've made my way through it all, somehow, but…like, what's my goal here, really?"

"Your goal, Yusa?" asked Chiho, eyebrows raised.

Emi shrugged, dejected. "You know, Chiho: I'm the Hero. I have the hopes of mankind on my shoulders. And, you know, the reason I came to Japan in the first place—"

"Currryyyy…mnngh…"

"Hee-hee! ……Sorry."

Maou couldn't help but laugh at the topic Alas Ramus chose to bring up as she talked in her sleep. It was like she chose it on purpose. A sharp glare from Emi, up in front, made his apology uncharacteristically meek.

"…The reason I came here was to slay the Devil King for trying to conquer Ente Isla. Or that's what it was supposed to be, anyway."

Her glinting eyes turned toward the withered Maou as she spoke.

"I am aware of that much," Suzuno added, still puzzled, "but how is that connected with any desire to return home?"

"Well…" Emi began, turning back forward, since Maou wasn't giving her any further reaction. Her eyes settled down on the baby in her arms, now in a deep and self-assured sleep. "Then Alas Ramus came along, so I couldn't just go slashing at the Devil King any longer…and then all these angels and demons came raining down on us like hailstones. Trying to get all of us mixed up, you know?"

"True enough."

"Kind of funny to think that us three're the only humans in this whole mix, huh?"

Chiho's observation was ignored.

“So all these outside forces that weren’t involved at all before I came here are sticking their noses in my business, and I’m getting sick of it. I just figured that...you know, maybe I should try going back to Ente Isla once. They can mess with me all they want to over there.”

“So you’ll come back and beat up all the bad guys?”

“Oh, how should I put it...?” Emi replied, dubious about how directly Chiho had decided to frame it. “I mean, it’s like all these different guys have been after my holy sword since right around when Bell showed up, right?”

“Indeed,” Suzuno interjected. “Lord Sariel was verily obsessed over it at first.”

“But that’s because it had to do with Alas Ramus, isn’t it?”

The archangels Sariel and Gabriel had both publicly proclaimed to Emi that they wanted to extract the Better Half from her—by force, if necessary. Ever since they’d learned that the sword had a Sephirah fragment at its core, heavenly forces had been trying hard to collect it as part of their quest for Yesod pieces—bits of which formed the very root of both the Better Half and Alas Ramus. Everyone here now knew that. But it didn’t mean they had to like it.

“Right, and the angels are one thing, but that demon Ciriatto was gunning for Yesod fragments in Choshi, too. It’s looking a hell of a lot like the Malebranche forces on the Eastern Island right now have a Yesod piece or two. And Erone’s another fruit of the Sephirah, and yet he’s tagging along with a demon.”

“I suppose the easiest way to explain it,” deadpanned Suzuno, “is that the heavens are connected to the demons somehow.”

“Wh-where’d that idea come from?”

The three girls turned around at once to find a peevish Maou squirming under their gazes as he strolled along.

“Yeah,” Emi said, “how are we gonna explain *this* guy, then?”

“True. The Devil King failed to even realize that Alas Ramus was born from the Yesod fragment he once possessed. And I fail to see any plausible motive for the heavens to side with the Malebranche forces that sprang up after the Devil King’s demise.”

"Look, I dunno what you're talking about, but would you mind not killing me off, please? I'm just fine!"

"So I was thinking," Emi said, ignoring Maou's Devil King status report. "We have too little to go on with Erone—and Gevurah, too—where *he* fits in. On the other hand, we kinda know a lot about Yesod at this point. So why do you think Sariel and Gabriel are so hot after Yesod *fragments*?"

"Huh?"

Chiho arched an eyebrow, failing to see Emi's point.

"Hey, uh, we're about to reach the station, so…"

Maou, meanwhile, continued to be ignored.

"I mean, why is it only Yesod that's been broken into fragments? They're only collecting those fragments because someone broke it and spread the pieces all over the place."

"Talk about a pain in the ass," Maou threw in, knowing that nobody was listening. Spotting a soda can on the street, he picked it up to toss it in the garbage can next to a nearby vending machine, only to find it full. He opted to perch it on top of the can lid instead.

"Oh… Now I get it."

"Huh?"

Suzuno nodded confidently to herself, much to Chiho's confusion. Emi, meanwhile, used her free hand to point a finger at Chiho's hand.

"…Oh!"

The hand had a ring on it that housed a single small, purple gemstone. It was a Yesod fragment, just like the one in Emi's sword and on Alas Ramus's forehead.

"I don't know for sure who broke it, but if we're talking about who scattered the pieces, I think that's pretty clear right now. We've got this one right there, besides."

During the whole rigmarole that led to Chiho obtaining this ring, she also had certain memories implanted into her mind. Memories of a faraway world that Chiho could never have comprehended. One from the past, perhaps. A small, wounded demon, and a man standing in a field of wheat.

"Your…mother, Yusa?"

"Yep. Pretty much." Emi rolled her eyes as she took her hand away. "So I thought maybe I could track her footsteps on Ente Isla from back before I was born, or when I was still too young to remember anything. Like, maybe that'd help me find something, you know? I'm not expecting miracles, but if something pops up, then great."

If Emi could turn back time, there was one regret she had wanted to right for a while. After Emeralda and Albert came to rescue her from Urushihara and Olba, she had a chance to revisit Ente Isla—a chance she wished she could've taken, even for a short time. Laila, Emi's mother, had apparently lived with Emeralda for a short time.

But Emi didn't take the chance. She had no allies on Earth at the time, and leaving the Devil King alone for a moment was unthinkable. Even if he didn't do anything nefarious, if he decided to move addresses while she was gone, it'd be back to square one with her search. After having spent nearly a year living by herself in Japan, there was no way she'd toss all her progress down the toilet that way.

She absolutely couldn't ask Emeralda and Albert to keep an eye on him, either. Emi was a simple farm girl at the core, but they both had high positions in government. Once peace returned to human society, they would have responsibilities to live up to. In a Devil King–free world where the old Church and nation rivalries were about to be rekindled anew, their talents were sorely needed back home, not on another world. Plus, by the time the demons were routed from Ente Isla, Emi's strength was at a level such that it'd take Emeralda, Albert, and Olba taking her on together to have half a chance at defeating her. Lucifer—Urushihara—had survived the fight under the Shuto Expressway, but practically speaking, if it came down to a fight against three arch-demons, Emilia the Hero was the only one capable of dealing with that.

If only Chiho had been a more important presence in the demons' lives earlier. If only Suzuno had arrived a little bit sooner. Emi knew it was pointless to wish for that, but she wished it anyway. Instead of that, Chiho had spent the past half year building a solid emotional relationship with Maou and his friends. For that matter, Suzuno wouldn't be in the picture in the first place, if Urushihara and Olba hadn't made that power grab. It was all this happenstance, all these little mistakes and mistimings, that kept things from going the way Emi needed them to go. Not that she could do anything about it.

Besides:

"*Ngh...mmmhhh...* We going home, Mommy?"

Somewhere along line, they had arrived at the Sasazuka Station turnstile. The noise from the PA system and the passing trains must have woken Alas Ramus up. She wrinkled her face as she took in the surroundings, her sleepy eyes turned upward.

"Oh, you up, Alas Ramus?" The sharp-eyed Maou, quickly noticing this, approached her to grab one of her hands. "Hey, come visit me again real soon, okay?"

Chiho and Suzuno waved behind Emi, flashing bright smiles.

"See you later, Alas Ramus!"

"Be a good girl on the way home, now."

The situation made Emi think a bit. If everything had gone the way she wanted, there probably wouldn't be any soft, gentle moments like these. Lately, she had started to think that maybe this wasn't so bad after all.

"Sorry I didn't get to play with you too much today, kiddo. I'll make up for that next time, okay?"

"Okeh! Promise!" The now-wide awake Alas Ramus thrust her hand toward Maou. Sticking out a single index finger was still too fine a motor skill for her.

"Sure thing. Promise."

"...What were you doing today, anyway? I almost never see you use that computer."

It was a surprise for Emi, seeing something take priority over Alas Ramus for Maou during her visits. Maou would never forget to take time out for her normally, no matter what.

The answer wound up coming from an even more surprising source.

"Well," Chiho stated, "Maou's gonna need to get a license soon."

"A what?" This was apparently news to Suzuno as well. She gave him a look. "You mean a…driver's license?"

That was what the term usually meant. It was hard to imagine Maou gunning for, say, an airline pilot's license at this point in his life. As far as Japanese law was concerned, he was an adult and therefore had every right to apply for one—but that wasn't what concerned the girls.

"And Alciel gave you permission for this?"

"Color me…*impressed*."

"Oh, *that's* the part you don't believe?" Maou's face soured. "Who do you guys think he is to me, anyway?"

"Yeah, but getting a license costs money, doesn't it? You have to go to driving school and all that, no? Do you have that kind of cash? Are you even planning to follow traffic laws in the first place? You *are* the Devil King, right?"

"Indeed," Suzuno added. "You know those young men that hand out tissue packs advertising driving schools in front of the supermarket or whatnot. The programs for even the cheapest of them start at a hundred thousand yen or so, am I right? I sincerely doubt Alciel would allow such an outlay, and I even *more* sincerely doubt you have the patience to save up such an amount, either."

"Why do I have to get all this abuse just because I said I'm getting a license, huh? What's so bad about the Devil King being licensed?"

"The idea of the Devil King seeking permission from government authorities to do anything is laughable."

As Emi said this, Suzuno eagerly nodded at her logic.

"Geez, guys," a defeated Maou spat out. "I didn't say I was getting a car license or anything."

"Oh, so what, then?"

"Something special?" Emi asked. "I've never seen you show an interest in anything besides MgRonald stuff. Something related to cooking or hygiene or something? Those cost money too, y'know."

"I'd like to get my food hygiene specialist certificate sooner or later, but…"

"I knew it."

"I might need it if I go full-time, is all I'm saying. But that's not it." Maou coughed, trying to regain control over the subject, then puffed his chest out. "So get this—I'm gonna apply for a motor scooter license!"

The sound of an express train roaring through Sasazuka Station passed above his head.

"...Okay, I better get going, girls."

"Have a safe trip."

Emi walked right past Maou, his chest still puffed out.

"Oh, come on, guys!" Chiho protested. "You could at least give Maou some kind of reaction! He's about to cry!"

"Aww..." Emi groaned. That was a tough order to follow, even if it came from Chiho. "I mean, all that lead-up, and that's...it? Not to pick on motor scooters or anything, but—Chiho, what kind of license do you think a Devil King would really want to get?"

"Um...? Well..." Chiho paused, not expecting this query.

"Guys, listen to me for a sec! I'm not just getting that license, either! It costs 7,750 yen to apply, and the company's covering up to 5,700 yen of that! How could I say no to that, huh? And not even Ashiya could say no when I explained where the remaining 2,050 yen would be going!"

"..."

Those old, familiar pangs of concern, the voices in Emi's and Suzuno's heads wondering how serious the Devil King was truly being half the time, wriggled back to the surface. They knew he was being 100 percent straight with them, and the realization made them both feel profoundly empty inside.

"...They could've covered the whole thing, at least."

"They're just covering the training costs! They can't pay the actual license fee for me! Company regulations!"

"Wait. By 'company,' you mean MgRonald, yes? Why would MgRonald pay you just so you have the right to haul your sorry hide around on a motor scooter?"

"Ah, I'm glad you asked! So the Hatagaya MgRonald location I am so proud to work—"

"We're starting a delivery service," Chiho said, attempting to hurry things along a little. "So all the staff twenty years old and up have to get scooter licenses. If you don't have one, the company's helping pay for the costs a little."

"..."

"Delivery? You mean...food?"

"More or less, yes," Chiho replied to an astonished-looking Suzuno. "We can't make deliveries on bicycles or anything, so we need licenses for the scooters. I'm still a teenager, so they wouldn't cover any of my costs, but..."

"I'm surprised to hear that," Emi said. "Didn't you just open a café upstairs? It's only been a couple weeks and you're rolling out something new already?"

"Yeah, Ms. Kisaki wasn't exactly a fan of that part of it..."

Mayumi Kisaki, crackerjack store manager at the Hatagaya Station–facing MgRonald Maou and Chiho worked hourly jobs at, was a woman so devoted to her job that she had earned the nickname "sales demon" from her coworkers. In her eyes, it was a given that daily sales had to be double what they were at the same time last year. Having this new delivery system rolled out when MagCafé was still such a new presence in town was currently giving her migraines.

"They picked us in kind of a hurry," Maou continued. "We're near a big metro highway, we're close to offices and residential areas, and we're one of the few sites that can do delivery on MagCafé items, too. It's not that things are going too fast, so much as we're totally short on people to carry 'em out right now."

The idea behind MgRonald's delivery system wasn't exactly new. Fundamentally, it was identical to the local pizza joint—if you're within the delivery zone and willing to spend at least 1,500 yen on an order, just call up the local MgRonald and tell them about it. The system had been gradually rolling out across Tokyo, starting with restaurants close to major highways, and Hatagaya's number just came up.

There was just one problem, though: The location was in no position to take on the job yet. Only a few employees had licenses at all, part of the reason Maou was so fervently studying for one right now. And the head count at the location was far too paltry to currently provide any kind of decent delivery service. They had a café counter upstairs to staff alongside the regular one, which meant more manpower that had to stay inside the restaurant at all times. They'd need to invest in multiple delivery vehicles, too. And they'd need either to hire on employees to take phone orders or to train everyone on how to do *that*, plus they'd need time and people to handle that job. And since orders wouldn't necessarily come from well-known streets all the time, they'd need a delivery team with a working knowledge of the local area.

For any of it to work, they needed to bring on some new talent ASAP. And considering the time Kisaki would need to train them up to her quality standards, the two months they had until the delivery program's November debut seemed to offer very little room for mistakes.

"Three more people," Kisaki had taken to muttering under her breath as of late. "I just wish I had three more people here at all times. Two, even!"

Two part-timers would be enough, in her mind, to keep the shifts full while training a new delivery team. But autumn was on people's minds now, and school would be back in session soon for college students—not a favorable time to try and beef up the staff.

"Hey, uh, you looking for a career change, maybe, Emi?"

Maou was only half serious. Emi sniffed at it anyway.

"I'm making seventeen hundred yen an hour right now, you realize."

"...Never mind."

"S...seven..."

The number floored Chiho, who—as an underage employee—didn't see much of any salary bump after her probationary period ended.

"Hey, I have to earn that salary every day, you know? It's hard. And I'm a Hero with years of combat experience under my belt, so I know."

"Y-yeah," Chiho said, "I know call centers suck sometimes."

For her job, Emi took customer-support calls for a major mobile phone provider in Japan. A call-center job could involve a lot of things—the subject matter you dealt with, whether you were making or receiving calls—and while it wasn't a given that the job was tough, Emi had a pretty stressful one, it seemed like.

Maou turned to Suzuno next. She cut him off before he could say anything.

"I am not interested, Devil King. I lack any confidence that I could master customer service and all that unfamiliar terminology to the degree Ms. Kisaki would no doubt demand of me."

Maou doubted any of the terminology was really that exotic. But, then again, this was Suzuno. She had that crusty schoolteacher vibe every time she opened her mouth. Picturing her chirping, *Good morning! I'm ready to take your order whenever you like!* with a permanent smile etched on her face was impossible for any of her acquaintances.

"Are all of you thinking something...rude about me right now?"

Suzuno was sharp enough to pick up on the pained expressions across every face. She glowered at her fellows as they quickly plastered on fake smiles.

"Well, regardless," Emi said. "Sorry I can't give you too much advice, Chiho, but hang in there, all right? Getting back to the subject..."

"...What were we talking about again?"

Suddenly, they all realized that they had spent the past twenty minutes talking in front of the turnstile. They froze for a moment. It was an odd sight—the Hero and Devil King completely losing track of time as they bounced from topic to topic.

"We were talking about me returning home. I've already requested time off from my company, so all I have to do is have Eme handle the details for me. I'm planning to leave at the beginning of the week."

"Whaaa?" Chiho gasped.

"This is rather fast, is it not?" Suzuno protested. "Maybe you think

I can handle things alone here, but there are so many preparations I must make in order to..."

Her eyes turned to Maou, who stood next to her. She paused, then put down the arms she had lifted in front of her for protest.

"...I suppose there aren't, are there?" she said, giving a solemn nod to Emi.

"See? Of course not."

"I don't know what you're talking about," Maou felt obliged to respond, "but I *do* know you're making fun of me by now."

"We're not making fun of you. We're complimenting you. You're diligent, serious, and you follow every rule in the book."

"Indeed. You rise with the morning sun. You are a staunch advocate of frugal living. You pour your blood, sweat, and tears into your labors, and you even engage in active study in order to adhere to the laws of our nation. Who would ever dare to make fun of that?"

"You could at least look me in the eye when you say that!"

"Wow, Daddy! You're really good!"

"...Thanks, Alas Ramus."

No one could defy the child.

"B-but Yusa, if you're leaving next week, then..."

Chiho stopped, too nervous to continue. Emi nodded, understanding what she meant, and gave a light snicker.

"Oh, it's all right. I don't want to bother people for too long over there—and I'd like to keep my job, too. I'll be back next weekend. I haven't forgotten what's happening on the twelfth."

"Oh, okay. Thanks!"

"The twelfth... Oh, right."

Maou and Suzuno nodded in understanding.

"And lemme just make it clear," Emi said while eyeing Maou intently, "please don't make it all weird for us, okay? Bell's one thing, but..."

"Aw, you're no fun," Maou replied, feigning ignorance. "I was planning on making her a Great Demon General badge or something, too."

September 12 came on a Sunday this year, and following intense lobbying from Chiho, the gang had decided to hold a tandem birthday party for both her and Emi on that day. Earth and Ente Isla ran on different calendars, but Emi knew she had been born in the early fall. Chiho's birthday was actually on the tenth, but that was a Friday, and Maou, whose attendance was an absolute must in Chiho's mind, worked the closing shift that night. So, they decided on the twelfth as a compromise. Planning things around the schedules of multiple people was never easy for them all.

"If you don't mind me ripping it to shreds the moment I see it, then sure, go ahead. Besides, part of the reason for this trip is to see whether all that crap you blurted out had any permanent effect over there or not."

Emi pouted at Maou. She had a right to. For all she knew, Ente Isla was now assuming as a given the fact that the Devil King was alive, his Demon General right-hand man was with him, and he had just appointed Emilia the Hero, Crestia Bell from the Reconciliation Panel, and the cashier from the local fast-food joint as his new top officers. Perhaps he had to—it was the best way handy at the time to keep Chiho alive—but Emi and Suzuno would have much to gripe about if the news set Ente Isla ablaze in speculation.

"I told you, it's all fine. Probably."

"I do *not* trust you on that!" Emi looked at her watch as she sighed at the offensively optimistic demon. "Oooh, I really better get back soon. It's almost Alas Ramus's bedtime."

"You're putting her to sleep this early?"

"She's been whining at me to take baths with her ever since we trained in that bathhouse with Chiho. She likes it hot, too. By the time I get it hot enough and spend some time in there with her, it's practically ten o'clock already."

"Hmm," nodded Suzuno approvingly. "Indeed. The very picture of a dyed-in-the-wool Tokyoite."

"Tokyoites don't come from Sephirah," Maou grumbled.

"I guess Erone would come from Hokkaido, then," Chiho added for no great reason. "All those layers he was wearing and stuff…"

"…All right. I really gotta go, so… See you on the twelfth."

“Oh, um, Yusa?” Chiho called out just as Emi was removing her rail-pass holder from her shoulder bag. “Would it be all right if I got to see you go? ’Cause I’m kind of worried…and besides, it’d be nice to say hello to Emeralda for the first time in a while, if she’s around.”

“I’m sorry, Chiho, but I promised Eme I’d go over on Monday afternoon, and you’re gonna have school, so…”

“…Oh.”

It was easy to forget at times, but apart from her skills at cross-planet, cross-species diplomacy, Chiho was just another urban teen. Emi gave the disappointed girl a pat on the shoulder, Alas Ramus joining her by batting her fat hand against her forehead.

“But don’t worry, all right? I’m the strongest Hero in human history, remember? And I’ll have Alas Ramus with me. I’m not planning on fighting or going anywhere dangerous. It’s just a quick trip to check up on the family home, pretty much.”

“Oh! Right!” Suddenly, Maou rushed right up to Emi. It seemed that only now did he remember that she and Alas Ramus were literally inseparable from each other. “I don’t want anything bad happening to Alas Ramus, got it? Just say hello to Emeralda, do lunch or whatever, and get her back here.”

Emi glared at him, deflecting his bravado back at him. “Where do you get off, telling me that? You’re the whole cause of this in the first place! And you better not try anything funny while I’m gone, either! Anything! Suzuno’s gonna have her eye on you the whole time, okay?!”

“Hah! Funny! You sure won’t be laughing by the time I get my license! I’ll have an entire new world to explore. Nobody can stop me now! You’ll be crying into your cereal by the time you get back!”

“I hope you forget to put the tax stamp on your application and they boot your ass out of the DMV!”

“Pfft! They sell those at the DMV, too! Try again, knucklehead!”

“Dahh!” Suzuno shouted as she forced her way into the inane argument. “Just go already, Emilia! You’re keeping Chiho and the Devil King here for too long! You have to stop before our holy scripture has to be rewritten to include the tale of how the Hero and the Devil battled over how to pay for a motor scooter license!”

Fifteen more minutes had passed since Emi last checked her watch. Between keeping Chiho out late and letting the baby stay awake, it wasn't an ideal scenario for anyone.

"You have nothing to fear, Chiho," Suzuno continued. "Perhaps it is not something to brag about, but I have little to occupy my time. I will be there with Emilia when she crosses over—I had wanted to speak with Emeralda myself. Is that quite all right, Devil King?"

The station's PA system squawked to life, announcing the imminent arrival of the next train. Emi turned her head up. "All right," she said, trying to hurry things along. "See you next week, Chiho. I'll send you a text later, Bell." And with that, she finally went through the turnstile.

"Bye-bye! Daddy, Chi-Sis, Suzu-Sis, bye-baah!"

As Alas Ramus waved with all her might from behind Emi's shoulder, the three of them feel tremendously guilty.

"I wasn't lying, though. They really do sell those tax stamps at the DMV."

"It doesn't… *Ugh.* I need to walk Chiho home. Are you all right time-wise, Chiho?" Suzuno asked.

"Oh, sure, no problem there…but…"

"Hmm?"

Chiho looked up at the sound of the train Emi and Alas Ramus presumably just clambered aboard, now leaving the station.

"Yusa's kind of been a lot more…cheerful lately, hasn't she?" she whispered.

"…Why're you looking at me?" Maou protested, a little self-conscious.

"What, don't you know?"

"Know what?"

Suzuno sighed as she pushed them both forward. "…We can walk and talk at the same time, you two."

"I really do think she's gotten more cheerful, though. Like, she's just a ball of energy right now."

"Ah, she's always been that way. Just whine, bitch, and moan, day in, day out…"

"Oh, Maou, I don't mean it *that* way! It's just...I don't know how to put it..."

"She said it herself," Suzuno said as she looked back toward Sasazuka Station. "About how it was better to seize the initiative on matters instead of waiting for something to happen. It has changed her outlook in all manner of ways, no doubt."

"Yeah, it's sure different from when she was all hesitant and going nuts over what she should do..."

It seemed even to Maou that Emi's happy, almost eerie sense of optimism—something she had back when they first met in Japan—had rekindled itself a little over the past few days.

"But it can't be just that, though."

"Oh?"

"What do you mean, Chi?"

"You really don't know, guys...?" Chiho gave Maou, then Suzuno a look of astonishment. "You two have the most to do with it, too."

All the two of them could do was exchange awkward glances. Apart from living in the same apartment building, Maou and Suzuno had nothing in common. That was especially true when it came to their involvement with Emi: Save for the fact they all lived in Japan, their relationships couldn't have been more different.

"Well," Chiho continued, "I'm not as involved as you are. And I wish I was. So I'm not gonna tell you!"

"Wh-what?"

"Um...?"

The two of them were forced to watch Chiho glare at them, looking a little triumphant as she did.

"All right, Chiho, I give in," Suzuno breathed as she lifted her hands into the air. They were nearly at the girl's house. "What have you discerned?"

Chiho turned her head back at her and smirked a little. "I don't know how much Yusa herself is aware of it," she said as she turned the rest of her body toward Suzuno. "But we're talking about the Hero who came here to slay the Devil King going back home, right? Doesn't that mean that she really trusts both of you?"

Maou and Suzuno both let out startled gasps.

"Yusa's convinced there's no way you're gonna do anything mean in Japan just because she takes her eyes off you for a few days. Even if you did, she trusts *you* enough, Suzuno, that she figures you can handle it. I think this is her way of saying that to all of us. Don't you think? Although I guess we're talking about a different kind of trust and stuff, but..."

This struck the both of them dumb. They were unable to react.

"Well, thanks for taking me home!" Chiho smiled a little and waved as she walked up to her door. "Say hi to Emi for me when you see her off, okay, Suzuno?"

Maou and Suzuno kept standing there for a few moments. Their eyes met, and then they shrugged and turned their backs to each other.

"That's not good, from the Devil King's perspective."

"...And let's just leave it at that, shall we? ...I'm going home. All this idle chatter has made it tremendously late. You would not want to stir Alciel's ire, would you?"

They exchanged no further words as they walked back to the apartment and silently went to their respective rooms.

"Welcome back, Your Demonic Highness! Ah, what a breath of fresh air this is, not having Emilia breathing down our necks! Shall we kick back and pay a visit to that *yakiniku* place, perhaps?"

Ashiya was acting quite out of character. If his idea of something to do when the Hero was gone was sitting around a griddle and cooking up bits of beef and pork, Maou mused, it might already be too late for both of them.

"My liege?"

"Oh, hey, Maou, did you get my text? I asked you to grab some custard for me at the convenience store on your way back home."

"...You did? Guess I didn't notice." Maou took out his cell phone, only to find a twelve-minute-old message waiting for him.

"Aw, duuude!" Urushihara grumbled. "Ashiya said it was okay for a change, too!"

"Damn it, guys..."

"My liege?"

"Hmm? Somethin' up, Maou?"

The way Maou was still standing bolt upright at the door unnerved them both a little. Maou paused, then lifted his face up. It betrayed his anger, an uncommon emotion for him as of late.

"The Hero's gone, and all you're going on about is meat and custard? See, *this* is exactly why Emi's put so much trust in us, guys! Where the hell is all of your Demon General *pride*, huh?"

The shouts from Maou, and the subsequent wailing and moaning from Ashiya and Urushihara, were clearly audible through the wall. Suzuno scowled to herself, hands over her ears, as she rode out the storm.

"As if *he* is in any position to talk..."

The Devil King next door, forced to chide his subordinates over *yakiniku* and cheap desserts, had clearly been poisoned by the everyday objects of Japanese society. And as Suzuno found herself forced to listen to an all-too-typical family argument from beyond the wall, she suddenly recalled a conversation she had with Emi a few days ago.

"The angels were human all along. In which case..."

What were demons, then? Especially the demon next door, currently studying the traffic laws of Japan in order to obtain a motor scooter license, and also a little frantic at the idea that the Hero and his unrequited crush trusted him.

Certainly, between Maou and Ashiya, demons certainly looked quite a bit more unhuman than angels. Unlike the denizens of heaven, who harnessed holy magic to materialize their wings, they were often of enormous size and sported things like pointy tails and horns that humans would never have. A few of them—such as Camio, the avian Devil's Regent who showed up in Choshi—hardly resembled humans at all.

But Suzuno had seen the Devil King Satan, the Great Demon General Alciel—even Farfarello, top officer in the Malebranche—in forms that were no different from any man or woman on the street.

"Perhaps I could investigate what that…*means*, exactly."

She sprang to action, grabbing her cell phone—but then stopped, shaking her head. It wasn't that her trust in Emi was gone, but having her go off by herself to see how things were on Ente Isla painted too murky a picture for her to be comfortable with. Casting too wide of a net would make it easy to overlook matters—matters that might impact Japan, and Chiho, in unpredictable ways. Emi said she was looking for clues leading to her mother—so why not let her focus on that, and that alone? The other mysteries unfolding in Ente Isla could affect the entire world. There was no point in hurrying things along too quickly.

The real issue right now, after all, was…

"Ugh, enough of this bickering! Settle down before I file a noise complaint!"

…She needed to quell the chaos next door as soon as possible. The flustered, frustrated Maou; and the quivering Ashiya and Urushihara…it wasn't a position she enjoyed. She knew that Emi entrusted her with watching over Devil's Castle for any suspicious moves, but…

"Stop your ridiculous arguing, start studying, and then go to bed! Don't you have work tomorrow?!"

…Intervening in a children's quarrel like a day-care supervisor wasn't meant to be part of the deal. She was starting to dread the next few days before Emi's return.

Walking back into her room, Suzuno closed the door with a hand behind her and let out a heavy sigh.

"Still…this *is* a form of peace and serenity, I suppose…"

It was wrong, yes, but it wasn't a bad thing. That was the simplest way of putting it.

❋

Monday rolled along surprisingly quickly.

After turning down an invite from her friends and wrapping up lunch early, Chiho was standing near the so-called chamber of horrors—the old school building that students and teachers usually never went near at all. She was staring intently at something in her hands. It was her ring, the small, purple Yesod fragment shining on top of it. As an upstanding, sensible high school student, Chiho couldn't bear having such a gaudy piece of jewelry on her finger during class.

Although no one had gotten around to explaining the process in detail, Chiho knew that "Gates" were a special sort of magic that let people traverse extremely long distances in an instant. Emi had gone through one to come here, and so had everyone else—Suzuno, Emeralda, Albert, Urushihara, Ashiya. Maou, too. And something told Chiho that when Emi and Alas Ramus went through their Gate this afternoon, this Yesod fragment would probably react to that in some manner or other.

She eyed the ring intently, making sure nobody else was around as she did. Then:

"...Ah!"

Suddenly, the fragment began to glow a dull purple. Then, for an instant, it sparkled brightly, like a camera flash, before fading and going back to a plain old gemstone. She had figured, with her magical training, that she'd feel some sort of force within her own body as well, but nothing special happened on that front.

There was, however, a new text on her phone. A simple notification from Suzuno: "Emilia has safely set off with Emeralda."

Emi, one of her best friends, was officially no longer in Japan. Or Earth, for that matter. It felt so strange to Chiho, who had yet to see a Gate being used in person. It was like Emi Yusa—Emilia Justina—was now just this kind of vague concept, neither extant nor gone forever, and it made her chest tighten.

Still, she said she wouldn't do anything dangerous, and Emi had Emeralda with her, besides. Any peril she might run into couldn't possibly be enough to overwhelm her, whether Chiho worried about it or not.

Chiho grasped her cell phone and closed her eyes as she recalled

Emi's phone number in her mind. Her hand, her ring, and the phone began to glow a little.

"Here's hoping the Ente Isla you return to is just a little bit more peaceful than it was before."

Would her prayer be strong enough to traverse Gates and worlds and dimensions? There was no way this novice spellcaster could know.

Even now, she didn't know.

Because after two weeks—after September 12 came and went—Emi still had not returned.

THE DEVIL
HAS AN
ENCOUNTER

Chofu Station was one of the main nerve centers of the Keio rail line, one where every type of train—from express to local—always made a stop. Keio trains going westward from Tokyo ended their journey either at Hachiouji and Mount Takao, or Hashimoto Station in the Kanagawa Prefecture city of Sagamihara—and Chofu was the point where they split toward one direction or the other. The front of the station housed a large bus terminal, offering connections between all of the local rail lines run by Keio, JR, and Odakyu.

It was still short-sleeves weather, but an advancing cold front in the afternoon meant there was a 60 percent chance of rain called for on this weekday.

Maou was there, departing the station through its northern exit.

"Umm… I think my stop's a little farther ahead…"

He searched for a certain bus stop—one he was at just the other day—only to find a line already forming at the spot he needed to wait at. The sign at the end read KEIO BUS: FOR TEST SITE FRONT GATE AND JR MUSASHI-KOGANEI STATION. He was just about to take a study guide out from his tote bag for some final brushing-up before the bus arrived, when:

"Mommy!"

Maou blinked, then instantly whirled around toward the voice.

There, he saw a young girl, hands extended out to grab the attention of her mother, who was studying a station map.

"..."

Maou didn't know them at all, but he still spent a moment staring at the pair. The mother traced a finger along the map a few times, then picked up her daughter. "All right, I'm sorry," she said. "Doing okay? Not too hot?" He could hear her continuing to speak as they quickly disappeared.

It was crowded around Chofu Station, but the vision of the mother and child remained on Maou's mind as he sighed and took his hand out of the tote bag. He knew there was no point to studying. He had already memorized every sample question in the *Conquering the Motor Scooter Exam* guidebook he'd purchased.

"Well, try number two, I guess..."

Maou shrugged as he grumbled to himself. He was headed for the Fuchu License Examination Center. Within the city of Tokyo, potential two-wheel drivers had their choice of three test sites, located in the Fuchu, Samezu, and Koto neighborhoods respectively. Today marked Maou's second visit to Fuchu this month.

"...Dammit, Emi," he whined.

As if on cue, the bus chose that moment to arrive. The line—either commuters or test takers like Maou, it seemed—filed into the vehicle and took their seats here and there, Maou being lucky enough to grab a free one near the door. He found himself reading through the exam-prep textbook again, despite himself. He couldn't afford to make another mistake. Not after he'd blown it last time.

A few days back, he had taken off one of his shifts, paid the city 300 yen for a certificate of residence, paid the local pharmacy 700 yen for the first ID photos he had shot since applying to MgRonald, paid Keio 170 yen for the one-way train ticket and a further 220 yen for the bus fare, and then capped it all off by failing the written exam.

When he realized his number wasn't on the electronic board showing the test results, he was gripped by a shock he hadn't felt since the news arrived that the Hero's group had laid waste to Lucifer's army on the Western Island. A shock perhaps more powerful than that, even.

He thought he'd had every question perfect. He had studied to the point where he could rattle off the exact wording of every law related to two-wheeled vehicles. He couldn't figure out where he went wrong.

Then he made the most pathetic little noise of his life.

"...Auh."

His superior memory skills, backed by his natural talent, effort, and demonic strength, reminded him of the cold truth.

"I put my answers in the wrong columns, didn't I...?"

The test was a basic true-false affair, with a couple of columns to the left of each question for marking in your answer. And while marking all your answers off by one column in a true-false exam would still earn you some correct answers, a passing grade in this one involved getting forty-five out of fifty questions right. There was simply no chance.

Thus, Maou's first attempt at scoring a driver's license was met with utter defeat. MgRonald added the costs of earning the license to your paycheck after you sent a request with a copy of the license—but, as was likely proper anyway, they only covered one exam. The abject sadness on Ashiya's face when Maou told him he'd have to pay 5,700 yen out of pocket instead of having the company cover it reminded him of the heartbreak when the Demon General advised him to abandon the Eastern Island following the humans' counterattack.

"...It's all that idiot Emi's fault," he muttered just as the bus's engines sprang into action, sending it softly forward after the driver issued one final "Everyone hang on, please" into the microphone.

"Why," he continued to himself, "does she have to get in my way all the time...?"

The past half month could be described in two simple words: *Couldn't focus.* Neither Maou, nor Ashiya, nor Chiho, nor Suzuno, nor anyone else. Urushihara, he couldn't tell.

Emi had departed for Ente Isla two weeks ago, on that Monday. Maou had work, Chiho had school, and Ashiya and Urushihara had no particular motivation to see Emi off. Suzuno said she was there, and around midafternoon she sent a simple text over to report that she was safely on her way.

Where she was headed was nowhere near Earth. And, of course, Emi had no obligation or reason to keep Maou and his demon cohorts abreast of her activities. Maou didn't bother doing anything on his end, figuring that Chiho or Suzuno were probably keeping tabs. He was too busy worrying about the upcoming driver's exam to pay too much attention to the people around him.

Things were peaceful. Mitsuki Sarue, manager of the Sentucky Fried Chicken across the street, was firmly devoted to his work. He was still eternally in love with Kisaki, manager at the MgRonald, and thanks to helping Chiho with her magical training, he was now able to interact with her on a regular basis again. A great leap forward—in his mind, at least—and he had been much friendlier with Maou and Chiho as of late.

Not having Emi griping at him all hours of the day was also doing wonders for Maou's work (and study) ethic. The sense of release was even affecting Ashiya's tight grip on their purse strings, to the point where there was always an additional item on the menu for dinner each night, and he didn't yell at Urushihara for ordering random crap from the Internet again.

Chiho was worried about Emi, of course. But, thinking logically about it, she was the strongest human being in the universe. It was clear that she'd be back soon and that it was useless dwelling on the subject, so Maou didn't bother trying.

❋

Things had started to change on Saturday that week.

"Has Emilia returned, Devil King?"

That was the question Suzuno had for Maou at the door to his apartment, asked before he departed for work.

"Uh? What're you talking about?"

"Oh, I just…wanted to see if she was back," she repeated before falling silent.

"I dunno," Maou said, a bit annoyed at being asked this. "She isn't?"

There would be no reason for Emi to notify him about her return. If Suzuno or Chiho didn't know, there was no way he'd know, either. He tried to explain this to Suzuno.

"Oh," she replied, her face a little troubled. "I see. I apologize for occupying your time."

"Mm?"

Maou and Ashiya exchanged confused glances with each other, while Urushihara was too passed out in front of the computer desk to respond. Suzuno went out to the hallway, pacing back and forth for a bit before finally summoning up enough resolve…to call Chiho.

"…Chiho? I apologize for calling so early," the demons could hear her say. As the conversation faded in and out of earshot, Maou took a glance at the shift schedule pinned to the refrigerator. It was Saturday, September 11, and if Maou's memory wasn't mistaken, Emi should have come home yesterday. The square for the twelfth had "Happy Birthday, Yusa!" written over it in Chiho's cutesy handwriting.

Suzuno's voice was no longer audible from outside. Just as he realized that, Maou's phone started ringing from the corner of the room he had tossed it to. It was from Chiho. She sounded ready to cry at any moment.

There was still no contact the next day. Maou had spent the previous day assuaging Chiho's worst fears, but even he was starting to think this was weird. Emi's personality was such that even if she didn't mind leaving Maou to stew in his own juices, she'd never do anything to make Chiho fret over her. Plus, today was the twelfth, Chiho's makeup birthday. Emi was a willing participant in that party, even if she didn't like Maou's presence there much. No way would she blow off that promise without so much as a "sorry."

Suzuno was back at Devil's Castle that afternoon, checking up on Emi's status. "Emeralda hasn't contacted you or anything?" Maou asked her.

"I am worried," she stated in a low voice from the hallway, "precisely because I cannot contact Emeralda, either."

On the roof of Emi's apartment building, when the Gate opened up two weeks ago, Suzuno had personally traded phone numbers and e-mail addresses with Emeralda Etuva, the most powerful sorceress on Ente Isla. They couldn't help but crack a smile about it—a Saint Aile court magician and a Reconciliation Panel cleric, two people who'd normally have zero contact with each other, using alien technology from Japan to do exactly that. Emi had used her own phone to send an Idea Link from Ente Isla indicating she was safe and sound at first arrival, which made her and Emeralda's current silence all the eerier.

Things on Ente Isla had gotten, if nothing else, much more complicated than back when it was simply mankind versus demondom. It was a huge mess of conflicting motives and power struggles, and it was nothing if not ironic that Emi's bringing peace back to the land was the trigger for it. For one thing, the world had fallen into a state of war between the Eastern Island and the other four landmasses that made up the planet. A group from the Malebranche tribe had infiltrated the island, hoping to resurrect the Devil King's Army, and they were being guided by Olba Meiyer, the Hero's former friend and someone who had once fought hard against demonkind.

That would make things knotty enough, but now the Malebranche were using an embodiment of a Sephirah—one of the core building blocks of the world and something the angels would do anything to recover. Secret maneuvering was taking place up in heaven, and only now was it bubbling to the surface.

Very few people know about all of that, but no matter how things turned out, Ente Isla's problems were definitely no longer the sort of thing that could be sewed up with a simple war or two.

"I fear relying on the Idea Link to contact Ente Isla too often. The waves of thought might attract the attention of the Church. That is why I hesitate to do anything too hasty."

The secret mission Suzuno had been tasked with was still technically in effect, even if she was no longer making any progress on it. Here, in Japan, she was taking the initiative to help the Church return to the just and proper organization it used to be, which meant she was now defying orders. Those orders commanded her to cover up Olba's activities—declaring to the world that the Hero was dead and even allowing the Devil King to do what he pleased. If that wasn't possible, she was to defeat both Emi and Maou, turning Olba's lies into a form of the truth.

Considering the two years it took for Emi to travel across the length and breadth of Ente Isla, no one at the Church nerve center expected Suzuno to fulfill her mission in the space of just over three months. But just because she wasn't the target of suspicion didn't mean she wanted them to know she was currently plotting against their will. The Malebranche on the Eastern Island, for all she knew, firmly believed that Crestia Bell was now a Great Demon General. Olba was apparently disengaged from the Church, so demon intel wouldn't fall into Church hands that easily, but either way, Suzuno's current position was quite a bit more unsteady than Emi's.

"There is every chance," she continued, "that people similar to how I used to be might be sent to Japan. People who would not hesitate to cause harm to Japan in order to dispose of the sorry truth behind Church doings."

"Yeah," Urushihara added. "Even before we came here, Olba was talkin' to me about how Emilia being alive was kinda a thorn in the Church's side, y'know?"

"Bell," intoned Ashiya, "listening to you speak, it sounds as though you decided to shelve that issue rather quickly after reaching Japan, did you not?"

"Perhaps," the unaffected Suzuno replied. "I have no defense for what Lord Sariel did...but, if I may be honest, you all bear the brunt of the blame for what happened."

"What?"

"...Or should I say, it was all your fault, truly."

"Now, I'm gonna have to object to that, lady..."

Suzuno was starting to get a little too arrogant for Maou's tastes. She simply shrugged at the jab.

"For me," she said, "the ideal resolution to all this would have been for Emilia to slay the Devil King in the world he fled to, bringing true peace to Ente Isla and guiding the Church back to something worthy of the faith after it heaped scorn upon the Hero's good name. But look at our Hero now." She let out a derisive sniff as she stared Maou down. "She truly believes you incapable of doing anything evil. Not only does she let you live, but she's even returned to her family home. At this rate, nothing will ever change with my current…situation."

Maou averted his eyes and clicked his tongue. This was getting awkward for him. Ashiya, for his part, let out a grumbling moan. Neither of them could counter her assessment.

"Things would change, of course, if I were allowed to smash all of you down. Right here, and right now." Suzuno squinted at Maou as he gritted his teeth. "…But, ah, now is no time for idle talk like that. Our problem right now is Emilia, and right now, there is nothing we can do from here. And if Emilia is incapable of returning home, it might be safer to assume that something's happened to Emeralda, not Emilia."

"Emeralda?"

"Indeed. Emilia is incapable of casting Gate magic, and neither can Emeralda, for that matter. Much of it comes down to the angel's-feather pens they have."

Maou's face wrinkled at the mention of the term. Nobody else noticed.

"It is Emeralda who takes care of those pens, so perhaps something has happened to her and Emilia is trying to do something about it… That is what I think, anyway."

Suzuno's hesitance was thanks to the fact that even she knew this was just idle speculation. It didn't take much of an effort from Maou to deflate it.

"Okay, so why isn't Emi telling you or Chi anything about this? She was chatting with Emeralda via Idea Link this whole time, wasn't she? It shouldn't be this hard for her to contact us. What's with the silence?"

"...If I knew the answer to that, I would not be in such a state right now." There was more than a twinge of frustration to her voice. "But what kind of trouble could have possibly befallen her? Because I am being quite honest when I say I cannot imagine what could possibly paint Emilia, of all people, into a corner like this. She is the Hero! Someone who flicked the Devil King's Army and an archangel away like so many flies! If we can no longer make contact with her, the only thing I could imagine is that the entire world was destroyed."

She was right: By both Earth and Ente Isla standards, there was no one that could be described as her equal. Much of that had to do with her holy force and the angelic blood in her, but even without that, it'd take a lot more than, say, an auto wreck to faze her. Even if she were faced with a foe on the level of the Church's order of knights, it wouldn't be close. Even against several of them. Even if they snuck up on her, and then bound and gagged her, too. Her holy force alone meant she could crush them without batting an eye.

"Hey, can I ask you something? Is it really that tough for human beings to conjure up Gates?"

Suzuno raised an eyebrow at Maou's sudden query. "What?"

"I mean, I know me, Ashiya, and Urushihara all look like this right now, but we all had the innate power to use Gates whenever we wanted. I guess Olba can, too, so I don't get why it's so impossible for you and Emi."

"Is that your way of bragging about your strength?" Suzuno closed her eyes, not appreciating the way Maou phrased it. "I *can* use Gates, technically speaking. And I suppose Emilia could as well, if she were trained for it. But it consumes such a vast amount of holy force, and it requires an extremely intricate spell to cast. Without that spell, and a suitable amplifier to harness it... Well, even if I could open a Gate, I'd be unable to venture through it, or be very sure of its destination."

"Oh, so it's a holy energy issue?"

"Quite. That is why Lord Olba is...extraordinary, in his own way. Summoning a Gate without so much as an amplifier is simply amazing. Even the six Bishops of the Church would hardly be a match for him—I suppose Lord Cervantes would have the best chance, thanks to his youth. Though whether even he has studied any Gate skills, I cannot say. It is not a spell that is called upon all that often."

"Yeah, I guess not..."

"There are several of us in the Church's diplomatic and missionary team capable of handling Gates, including myself, but Lord Olba is the only one I know of who can conjure them without an amplifier. And when I say 'amplifier,' I am speaking of enormous structures—Sankt Ignoreido, for example, the 'Stairs of Heaven' located at the assorted prelate sites on the Western Island. One would need to travel to one of those sites to access them, which is another reason why Gates are only rarely used by us."

"Huh."

"Of course, I have my doubts whether even someone like Lord Olba can form a complete Gate and perfectly define its destination through his own strength alone. If his real intention was to eliminate Emilia, after all, why would he send her to a human world with nations as rich as this one? He would not do that deliberately, no."

It made sense enough to Maou, at least.

"I should also note that opening a Gate is quite a different matter from stabilizing it and going through it. I could probably manage the opening process with no external aids, but no further. I would not be able to guarantee the safety of whoever went through. And were I the one doing the traveling, I would need to keep it stable while I journeyed onward. I have no idea how long that would take, but I would need to continually pump power into the Gate, or else it would destabilize and send me to who knows where."

"Oh..."

Maou and Ashiya turned and nodded to each other. They had to admit that it made sense. Losing control of their own Gate was the entire reason why they fell into Japan in the first place.

"Okay," Urushihara suddenly blurted out, "so if Maou here becomes the Devil King again, he can hop right back to Ente Isla, right? Like, we've already proven that he can convert holy force into demonic if you overload him with enough of it. Then he can open all the Gates he wants to, yeah?"

"Hmm," an astonished Ashiya said. "A surprisingly constructive observation coming from you, Lucifer."

Suzuno looked less impressed.

"Probably not, I'm afraid."

"Yeah, I don't think so, either," Maou added. "Emi was with us all last time. Now, it'd just be Suzuno. And she could probably drill all her holy force into me and it wouldn't make the demon force come back. It'd just make me feel a little sick to my stomach."

"I hate to admit it, but you are right. I have perhaps half of Emi's holy strength at best—our capacities are on a completely different scale from each other. If I put that into you and poisoned your demonic side with holy force, you would no doubt fall ill, lose your job, and be homeless within a month, no?"

"Oof," Ashiya said, newly concerned.

"Aw, I thought that was a pretty good idea, too," Urushihara whined as he leaned back on his legless chair.

"...Well, hang on a second." Maou waved his hand in the air. "Why are we treating it as a given that Emi's in trouble and I have to swing in to rescue her? 'Cause maybe you forgot, but I'm the Devil King, y'know? Her mortal enemy. I don't give a crap if Ente Isla starts a war with itself or whatever. Hell, that's great for me, actually. Plus, Emi knew the risk she was taking going back there, right? It's her problem now. Yours, too, I guess? I don't care. I feel kinda bad for Chi, but..."

Maou shot a glance at the schedule on the refrigerator, recalling Chiho as she wrote her message on it a couple weeks back.

"Not even the entire Devil King's Army could stop Emi," he continued, picking up his usual conversational speed. "And now that she's back in Ente Isla, her body's naturally recharging its holy force. She's gotta be several times stronger now than she was here, even. Isn't it kinda pointless worrying about her safety? And if *you* can't do anything, *we* really can't, either. The only difference is that we have no reason to care about how Emi's doing. She went there on her own volition."

"But…Devil King…"

"This conversation's over, okay? I'm assuming we're gonna cancel the party if she doesn't show today, so I'm gonna study for my license test tomorrow. Get outta the way, Urushihara."

Urushihara, unexpectedly for him, got the picture quick. He sidled away from the computer desk, giving Maou the space he needed to access a website with a selection of sample tests, giving every indication that he was done talking for now. Ashiya, Urushihara, and Suzuno gave him confused-looking stares.

"Devil King."

"…What? Are we not done here?"

"Would you say the same if Chiho asked you for help?"

"I…" Maou fell silent for a moment. But it didn't change his mind. "I'd phrase it a little softer than that," he said, back still turned, "but it's gonna be the same thing in the end. It's not like I'm some omnipotent god who can do anything. And we're talking about Emi, okay? Like I said, I don't see the point of worrying about her."

Ashiya and Urushihara found it impossible to reply. But someone else didn't.

"Maou…"

It was a small voice, ringing out across Maou's slumped back and his heart. It made him hold his breath as he turned around.

"M-Ms. Sasaki…"

"Oh, that's nasty."

Ashiya's groaned reaction, and Urushihara's pointed criticism of Suzuno, were both aimed at a small and clearly crestfallen Chiho. She was next to Suzuno, her eyes quivering with concern—and now she was turning them to Maou. That explained why Suzuno never actually entered the apartment—she wanted to be sure Chiho heard the whole thing.

"Chi…"

"Maou, I know you're not the kind of person to go back on your word."

"...Huh?"

It wasn't what he expected to hear. What he *did* expect had already made a chill run down his spine.

"I know you're the Devil King and she's the Hero. I know you're enemies and everything. And when you say that you don't care what happens to Emilia the Hero, I'm sure that's what you really think inside."

Her voice was shaking, hands clasped in front of her chest. So much as a poke would have made her start crying.

"I'm sure there's nothing we can do about the fact that the Devil King Satan and the Hero Emilia knew each other as enemies. I guess there wasn't any way of avoiding that in the first place. But... Maou... I mean, didn't you say it to me yourself? Didn't you...give me a really great present?"

Emotions Chiho could no longer contain were now spreading across her face.

"I...I think Emi might not like it much...but you, you told me, didn't you? You said that me...and Suzuno, and Yusa, were all your Demon Generals, didn't you? You said we could be with you, and you'd show us this amazing new world..."

"...Ms. Sasaki."

"Whoa, nobody told me about—*ow!*"

Ashiya, attempting to give Chiho's pained plea the serious response it deserved, instead found himself slapping Urushihara, for once again failing to get the hint.

"And you, Urushihara," Chiho continued as she watched him grasp his nose in pain. "You betrayed him once, but you're still a Demon General...*snif*... And you said her name, Maou... You named her...and nobody made you do it..."

"..."

"If it's pointless to...to worry about her, that's fine. It'd be better that way, even...but Yusa's so strong, and yet she's still gone...and I'm so worried..."

"Chiho..." Suzuno gave her a shoulder for support. Chiho's knees looked ready to collapse on her.

"And...and Alas Ramus is still with her, you know? How could you not be worried about her, at least...? I know you're lying about that right now... *Hooph.*"

Chiho sighed, relieved that she managed to scale the mountain of her emotions before they fully got the best of her. She gave the room a polite bow.

"Uh..."

"...I'll see you later."

She gave another bow and was just about to step behind Suzuno and walk back home when Maou let out a single, lifeless syllable.

"Chi..."

Chiho stopped. She didn't turn around. "...Yes?"

For a moment, Maou failed to understand why he had called for her. After a measured silence, he finally managed to get this out:

"...Don't do anything dumb like try to contact Emi with an Idea Link, okay? 'Cause if she's actually in trouble, that might put you in danger, too, Chi."

He knew it was insipid, but that was all he could say. And of course he couldn't see the human girl's expression with her back turned.

"All right," Chiho replied. Then she walked down the stairs and left Villa Rosa Sasazuka alone. Once the stair clanging ended and Maou saw Chiho round the corner with tottering, unsteady steps, he gave Suzuno a resentful glare.

"...Damn it, Suzuno..."

He had fallen straight into her trap. And Maou wanted to curse Suzuno for that, but he—and she—both knew how weak his facial expression was right now.

Suzuno all but chuckled in response. "It is what I had to do," she said, "to make sure you truly cared not at all. I, after all, was very reluctantly named a Great Demon General in your revitalized army. Why shouldn't I have my reporting general think about how to protect one of his top officers?"

"...Uh, does someone mind cluing me in on all this later?" the very peeved-sounding Urushihara said, as Suzuno watched him climb into the closet.

"No Great Demon General can rely completely on her commanding officer, of course. So, for now, all I want is a commitment."

"If you're gonna use your position only when it helps you, I'll happily strip you of your post, y'know. I don't see how I can make a commitment on any of this, besides."

"You sat there, slack-jawed, and said nothing to counter Chiho's words. That proved to us all that you are, indeed, concerned about Emilia and Alas Ramus's safety. What more commitment could I possibly ask for?"

Maou glared at her. "..."

"I am off. I need time to think about what I can do. After all, Chiho put it best—it'd be best for all of us if all this concern is for nothing."

Without another word, Suzuno departed from Devil's Castle.

"...Shit..."

Maou slapped a fist against the computer desk.

"Your Demonic Highness," said a voice from behind, "if I may..."

"*What?* Are you gonna bitch at me to think about her, too?"

"No, my liege. To be honest, my main concern regarded why you are still considering Emilia and Bell to be your Great Demon Generals...but I believe there is another, graver issue to consider."

"Yeah?"

Maou could tell from his voice that Ashiya had kneeled down behind him.

"I know you dodged discussing the possibility just now, but I believe the thought fully occupies the minds of both Bell and Ms. Sasaki. It is too easy for them to believe Emilia is in trouble."

"..."

A sample scooter-license test was still being displayed on the screen in front of Maou. It was on a picture of a road intersection from the viewpoint of a passing vehicle, next to some sort of question about predicting potential hazards. The test taker had to correctly answer a true-false question about what danger might ensue from the scene in the picture.

"It is true, my liege, that staging a full-frontal attack on Emilia ultimately led to the demise of the Devil King's Army. But now, the flames of war crossing Ente Isla are being fanned by human hands. There is no guarantee that the 'danger' dulling Emilia's blade and strength would be a sword stabbing at her from the front."

"..." No, there wasn't.

"Even after human society betrayed her, Emilia has still retained her pride as the Hero and savior of humanity. She has always attempted to pursue the path to true justice. If a fellow human wanted to restrain her powers, what would be the best approach to take?"

"...How should I know what humans are thinking?"

"Even now, my liege? After you resolved to stay in this world in order to investigate the human race's thought process?"

Ashiya's voice remained calm, but just like Chiho, he was poking right at the contradictions in Maou's mind that the Demon King was doggedly clinging to. He was up to the task, because he knew Maou better than anyone else in the world. Few subordinates are more valuable to a boss than the one capable of giving things to him straight.

"Apart from Emeralda Etuva and Albert Ende, it is safe to say that Emilia can call not a single soul an ally in Ente Isla. The power brokers in the Church are against her, Barbariccia and his Malebranche horde are against her...even the very heavens are against her. And if they learned somehow that Emilia has ventured into their own territory, I am certain they would be watching with bated breath."

Emeralda had undoubtedly done everything she could to keep a lid on it. But it was easy to imagine that both she and Albert were under constant surveillance by any number of forces. She herself had escaped confinement at the hands of the Church, publicly contesting them over their official position that Emilia the Hero was dead. That surveillance was going nowhere as long as Suzuno continued to fail to do the Church's bidding. If someone had picked up on Emeralda's movements and decided to act on them, what would happen if they set the sort of trap Suzuno was picturing in her mind?

"Well...I'd guess taking someone hostage would be easiest, wouldn't it?"

"Indeed, my liege. That may not necessarily be Emeralda Etuva. It does not matter who, really, as long as it makes Emilia hold her sword. If the person means enough to Emilia, they could serve as the perfect shield against her godlike force. Nothing could be more human, could it?"

"Yeah, no. The whole idea of a hostage didn't exist in the demon realms before I unified it, and none of the humans were ever goofy enough to take a demon hostage. But why would someone on Ente Isla want to go that far against Emi? She's still the savior of their world, isn't she?"

It seemed to Maou that nobody on Ente Isla had any reason to actively oppose Emilia the Hero. She had insurmountable strength. And what would lobbing stones at the savior accomplish for anyone?

"There is little we can do about it now, but... Your Demonic Highness, I fear that naming Emilia and Bell your Demon Generals when Farfarello left us was something of a blunder."

Maou gave Ashiya a look. It was a sore topic to him as well.

"When I heard about that," Ashiya continued, voice taking an admonished tone, "I thought at first it was part of an attempt to eliminate Emilia and Bell from our lives...but that was not the case, was it?"

Here we go again, Maou, thought. Back into lecture mode. His face tightened.

"Look, I know I was kinda caught up in the feeling and all back there, but I kinda had to, in a way. It guaranteed Chiho would stay safe, and it'd keep the demons from screwing around in Japan any longer. I mean, once Barbariccia knew Emi was alive, he was ready to attack Earth pretty much immediately."

Ashiya nodded.

Maou had enough respect for his demon citizens that he never wanted them to waste their lives in pointless wars. The encounter with Ciriatto in Choshi proved to the Malebranche's leaders that a face-to-face struggle against Emi would end in failure, whether she had all her force back or not. No matter what was motivating Barbariccia to step away from the demon-realm mainstream, neither

Emi nor Suzuno would be willing to have him actively meddle with Japan any further.

In order to eliminate that cause, Maou had to prove that the demon enemies of the past were no longer enemies. It was something he could only show him in Devil King form. And it was the correct approach. It was correct, but…

"Do you realize, Your Demonic Highness, that naming these three new Great Demon Generals comes at the expense of the safety of Japan and Ms. Sasaki, as well as the safety of Emilia and Bell in Ente Isla?"

Maou gamely opened his mouth.

"Um, what? We've got Suzuno and Emi here… Farfarello would've reported back to Efzahan about it… Barbariccia's firmly established in the Eastern Island…"

He waggled a finger into the air as he organized his thoughts.

"……Oh."

Then he brought a hand to his face.

"Ohhhhh, the humans are gonna be so pissed! They think Emi and Suzuno did a heel turn on them!"

"You truly did…not understand that?"

Ashiya sighed.

"I doubt they would believe it immediately, no," he continued. "The rumor would come from demon mouths, Emilia is supposed to be dead, and Bell's mission remains a secret one, as far as we know. But it would be more than enough to make the more doubtful of them take action."

Just like Suzuno said. A new assassin, perhaps, or a large army of humans. He thought he was rid of the demon threat, and instead he had inadvertently put Emi and Suzuno in danger.

"Okay, but…but in that case, why did they…?"

Suzuno had just called herself a Demon General, albeit half-jokingly. And apart from the first day, it seemed like Emi tolerated it, too, in order to keep Chiho safe.

"They accepted it, I am sure. They accepted the danger, too, I imagine, as a suitable risk in exchange for Ms. Sasaki's safety. Emilia resolved to return home, after all, because of the concerns she voiced about having to be more proactive, did she not?"

"...Well."

"They were both aware of those risks, and they said nothing about it. Out of respect for Ms. Sasaki, to some extent...but perhaps, I think, they wanted the status quo between us to be sustained. We remain in conflict, of course, but now we share our evening meals around the same table."

"And what do you think of that?"

"At this point, my liege, as long as you can fulfill your ultimate ambition to take over the world, it no longer greatly matters to me what approach you deign to take. I do find the idea of aligning with our bitterest of enemies rather disdainful, yes, but..."

Maou gave an annoyed look at Ashiya's barefaced rebuttal. Ashiya looked on with a half smile before quickly growing stern again.

"And I have been thinking, Your Demonic Highness... Which one of these forces is clearly seeking Emilia's physical body?"

"Huh?"

"Emilia possesses a strong body and an indomitable spirit. No regular human could force her to submit in any conceivable way. She would immediately seize the first opportunity available and slash right through it."

"What're you getting at?"

"Which one of the players here, my liege, sees value to Emilia apart from her strength in battle?"

"...Wait, are you kidding me?"

The faces of the many angels who had confronted him in their search for Emi's sword, Alas Ramus, and the Yesod fragments flashed back into Maou's mind. If her suspicion was right and Emilia was in trouble after all, the repercussions might even affect their adopted child.

"But that's all just speculation, isn't it?"

Suddenly, they heard a sliding door open. Urushihara popped out of the closet, carrying a drawer from the miniature chest he had installed in there without permission.

"I dunno if Ente Isla's and Earth's calendars are running at the same speed or whatever. And it's not like the horse wagons always come on schedule like the trains in Japan, y'know? Emeralda Etuva had to get the schedule aligned to make this visit work, so maybe they're just having a hard time getting the timing right."

Urushihara placed the drawer on the ground and fumbled through its contents.

"Not that we're ones to talk, but it's not like there's gonna be a ton of working infrastructure where they are. Not after our armies destroyed most of it. So maybe she's too used to things in Japan, so she wound up getting delayed over there."

"...Sounds pretty optimistic to me."

"Yeah, but Chiho Sasaki's being way too pessimistic. The day's not even over yet and she's probably crying her eyes out back home, dude. And you talked about never taking hostages, but my Western Island forces took a crapload of Saint Aile officials hostage. I mean, geez, we had Emeralda Etuva for a while. But that sure as hell didn't stop Emilia from saving them all and beating the crap out of us, y'know? It's kinda hard to think that, like, there's a hostage that's keeping her from acting at all."

There was something convincing about the argument, given that it came from someone who took on Emi twice and lost majorly both times. Emi certainly had enough pure strength to smash through whatever devious tricks someone might play on her.

"So, like, let's just try waiting a bit, okay? I get that you're worried about Alas Ramus, but you know she's gonna be fine as long as Emilia's still alive. At the very least, you know there's nobody here or on Ente Isla who could kill her right now."

Urushihara picked up the drawer, never removing anything from it in the end, and took it back to the closet before bringing out another drawer.

"Let's just wait and see what Bell tries to do. You know Emilia wouldn't want you to do anything for her anyway, right, Maou? Like, no matter how bad off she was."

It was true. If anything, doing too much for her would just make her all angry again.

"...Ashiya. Urushihara."

"Yes, my liege?"

"Mmm?"

Maou grinned a bit as he took a breath.

"Sorry about before. I'm a little calmer now."

Then he turned back toward the computer.

"For now, I'm just gonna focus on what's in front of me. Once she comes back, I'm gonna shove my license in her face and pick on her about being late. As much as I can 'til she snaps, y'know?"

"..."

"Sounds great to me, dude... Damn, where did I put it? He left it here last time... I don't think I threw it out."

Ashiya gave a silent bow behind Maou's back as Urushihara took out a third drawer, apparently searching for something.

Emi never made it back that day, either, but—on the surface, at least—it was just another day in Devil's Castle.

⁂

Thus, in the end, Maou found himself forced to take the exam a second time. He didn't want to play the blame game too much, but Ashiya's and Chiho's words for him had thrown off his concentration.

He had named Emi a Great Demon General, yes, and he also declared that he would help her find a new calling in life. And Ashiya wasn't just idly speculating, either. The heavens wanted Emi's body, and if they found out what she was up to, it was a given that they'd take a rather predictable strategy.

But after he attempted to wrest Emi's holy sword from her, Sariel's love for Maou's boss had turned him completely into a typical Japanese man. There was no sign he was staying in contact with the heavens at all. And Gabriel, just as powerful as Sariel, was no match at all for Emi. A tandem archangel strike might be one thing—but if they pulled something like that off, they'd have heard of it, whether it was in Japan or not. Ente Islans would be able to pick up on their holy force, which made it all the more perplexing that Emi wasn't back yet.

That was what dominated Maou's mind to the point that he put his test answers one column off from where they should have been. And now it was exactly two weeks since the day Emi was supposed to return home.

Suzuno had been working out her plans the whole time, evidently. She was in the midst of procuring an amplifier in Japan strong enough for the complex spell she had concocted to send an untraceable Idea Link. She had tried a few experimental sonar transmissions, and she was also trying to track down Albert, Emi's other friend. About everything she could do from Japan, Maou supposed. The effort meant that Suzuno's room was filled with strange-looking objects serving as amplifiers, as well as pages upon pages of magical incantations. It looked like she had signed on for some kind of cult, and so far, it had provided zero results.

The only thing they were reasonably sure about was that Emi and Emeralda were not back in Japan. The last Gate opened between Japan and Ente Isla was the one Emeralda showed up to control and Emi used to make her travels.

Chiho had grown increasingly taciturn during her work shifts. Kisaki, unaware of what had happened, even voiced concerns that Maou had made an indelicate pass at her again. And between the failed exam and the general weirdness of a life without Emi in it, Maou must have been acting differently as well.

"If you need to talk to me about something," Kisaki told him, "I'm right here, you know."

He shouldn't have had anything to discuss. His sworn enemy was gone. It was so freeing to them that Ashiya seriously suggested going out for *yakiniku*.

"Look, no," Maou told himself, recalling the results of the last test. "I'm just worried about Alas Ramus, is all."

A truly gifted liar lies only about the most important of matters.

Otherwise, he tries his best to tell the truth and avoid suspicion. Telling a lie to someone else is bad enough, but sometimes, the lies you tell yourself can be even more deceitful in nature. They eat at your soul, making it retreat inward.

It was true that he was worried about Alas Ramus. But Maou himself knew that it was more than that. And trying to weasel out of that with logic—feeling the need to weasel out of it at all—annoyed him.

"Next stop, Observatoryyyy," the bus driver said through the PA in the classic drone all public transit employees in the world use. The bus glided to a stop. They were about halfway between Chofu Station's north exit and the test center; this stop served the entrance to the National Astronomical Observatory of Japan, stationed in the city of Mitaka.

"Phew! We have made it!" said a haggard-sounding voice from the bus's rear entrance. Maou looked behind him to find a small woman in a pair of khaki overalls and a newsboy cap that almost covered her eyes being joined by a man in a business suit.

"C'mon, Pop, hurry!"

"Yes, yes… Oof."

They must have been father and daughter.

It hadn't occurred to him before now, but it turned out the name of the bus stop was pretty accurate. A gate was perched on top of a small, tree-lined hill, giving the area a university-like feel.

"Huh. So *that's* what's up there?"

Considering all the light pollution in Tokyo, the presence of an observatory so close by came as a surprise to him. Mitaka was a pretty big town, a bedroom community for Tokyo—something it had been for ages. He doubted anyone could see too many stars with the naked eye from here, at least…

That was about the extent to which Maou's brain could keep itself occupied with this new, unusual-looking presence. He decided to spend the rest of the trip studying.

"All aboard, please…"

With a jolt, the bus sprang forward. This bus stop was on a hill, and the resulting rocky start caused the study book to fall right out of Maou's hand.

"Oop."

"Oh?" said one of the passengers standing by him. The book had fallen right on her foot.

"S-sorry."

"Oh, no, it is good!"

It was the girl in the newsboy cap. For a moment, Maou felt a little awkward about reaching out to her body in a public area. The girl came to his rescue, deftly bending over without touching anyone else and handing the book back to Maou.

"Here!"

"Oh, thanks."

The cap was down enough over her face that Maou couldn't get a clear look at it, but she didn't sound angry, at least. In fact, she was smiling at him, hand outstretched. But…

"…"

"Ummm…"

Why was she staring so intently at the hand Maou was using to take the book? He grasped it now, but she refused to loosen her own grip on it. A little tug-of-war game was starting to ensue.

"Ummmmm…"

"…*snif.*"

Did she not hear him? No, she had to have. But she was still in that same position, hand on the book. After a moment:

"…*snif.*"

"Um, hey…"

She was trying to take Maou's hand, book and all, and bring it to her face. He was unable to surrender his book, but equally unable to accept this loony behavior, either.

"Hey, what're…?"

He pulled his hand back, only to have it grabbed by her own. Maou wasn't the type of young man to derive pleasure from this. They were in public, besides. He tried to wrest his hand back, instinctively trying to defend himself.

"I just need one of the moments."

"Huuuh?"

The girl refused to let go. Then—

"...*snif*."

She was smelling his hand?

"H-hey!"

This was getting too creepy even for Maou. He gave his arm another tug, this one stronger. This one was successful, although it meant giving up the book. Maou gave the girl a puzzled look, while she flashed a dissatisfied frown.

"Look, uh...the book, please?"

Maou really didn't want to talk to this disaster any longer, but he couldn't just give up something he bought with his own money. He had memorized every word of the book by now, so it had no value to him, but it was the principle of the thing.

Then...

"...Tsubasa."

A new voice called out to the girl.

"Yes, Pop!"

It was the man in the suit who joined her on the bus. Oh, right—they were related to each other. Looking at the presumable father, Maou could tell he definitely took good care of himself, although he clearly wasn't Japanese by race. Come to think of it, there *was* something a bit weird about the girl's vocabulary here and there. Maybe they'd immigrated here.

The father took the book from the girl he called Tsubasa and offered it to Maou again.

"Pardon us for the troubles."

"Oh, n-no..."

This guy seemed normal, at least, although Maou still wanted him out of his life ASAP. Maou opened the book and took his eyes away from the two of them, not bothering with politeness any longer. But:

"You apologize to young man, too, Tsubasa."

"Yes, Pop!"

In response to the father's misguided kindness, Tsubasa stretched her back straight and lowered her head to the point that it almost butted Maou's.

"I am sorry!"

She had a reason to be—but then again, this all got started because Maou dropped a book on her. "Nah, it's all right" seemed to be the right thing to say. The father nodded in response and turned away from Maou.

"..."

But the girl, after righting herself, stayed right there. He face was turned to him, as if watching his every move.

...This is so uncomfortable, Maou thought to himself. How much time was there until the test center? He scowled at the thirty-kilometers-per-hour speed limit sign out the window.

"Hey! Hey, sir!"

They weren't even at the next stop, much less the test center, and now this Tsubasa girl was talking to him! Why did this have to happen?! Maou couldn't hide the discomfort on his face any longer.

"Are you going to receive the license, too?"

"Uh, yeah... Yeah, I am, but..."

He was about to tell her off when he remembered her father was right next to him. It forced him to maintain at least a token effort at decorum. It sounded like they were headed to the same spot he was. Maou felt dizzy for a moment.

"How many failures?"

"Huh?" Maou turned his eyes way, not understanding the question.

"This is my and Pop's tenth test. World record!"

"T-tenth..."

Maou didn't know how to respond. That was a shockingly high number. As Kisaki and the rest of the licensed MgRonald employees told him, the written exam was a tad tricky and easily failable if you didn't know what you were getting into. Failing it nine times in a row, however, was hard to swallow. It probably *was* a world record, albeit one nobody would want published in a book.

"Um, could you quiet down a little...?"

Her father, the bearer of this record, was still right there. He might be a total stranger to Maou, but having this dishonor blared out for all the world to hear before they even reached the test site wasn't an auspicious way to kick things off.

"Yes, yes. So it goes, so it goes. Pop, he is not so good with the kanji yet..."

Maou didn't know if he was gunning for a regular automobile license or a scooter one like he was, but something told him that learning how to drive was the least of his problems. "So it goes" wasn't the half of it. And as for the father being so publicly put upon right now:

"...!"

"..."

Maou looked out the corner of his eye at him. Their eyes met for a moment, and once they did, Maou averted his and looked out the window. Or pretended to.

"..." *If you're listening,* Maou pleaded to himself, *at least say* something.

"So how many for you, sir?"

"Uh, this's my second time..."

"Wow! Cool. Just twenty percent of Pop!"

She was right, but to Maou, it sounded like the girl was comparing her father to him and finding the results severely lacking. He had to find a way to keep Tsubasa from slamming her father's good name.

"Uh, s-so are you taking a test, too?"

"Uh-uh. I'm his manager. Uh, his attendant? I'm attending Pop."

This was getting nowhere. What was she talking about? Was this girl going to stand next to her father during the whole exam? Wasn't it usually the other way around, if anything? That would be unusual enough, but...

"So...um, you aren't taking it...?"

"Oh, I was thinking about the taking!"

She could've just said that first, Maou thought. Test takers didn't need to reserve a spot in advance; it was open to anyone who showed up and filled out the application on time. Maou prayed internally that he wouldn't be sharing a test room with this pair.

"But I didn't study, so maybe I won't. Just attend Pop instead."

Maou began to feel fatigued. They were at least conversant in the Japanese language, but if he had failed the written exam nine times in a row, "Pop" must not be too good with the reading-and-writing part of things yet. Japan's DMV didn't just give out licenses to people off the street like this.

"Well, better luck next time…?" was the only thing Maou could come up with to say.

"I will do my best!" Tsubasa shouted, hands in the air. It would've been nice if that ended the conversation, but after a moment of silence and a single left turn from the bus:

"Hey! Hey, sir? Sir?"

"…What?"

She spoke up again.

Maou had given up on any further study on the bus, but thinking about how much longer this ordeal had to go on made him despair inside.

"What is your name, sir?"

"Umm…"

Maou's hesitation was wholly deliberate. Friendliness was fine and all, but this was not a relationship he wanted to foster at all. He honestly wondered whether giving a name would be a good thing or not.

"My name is A—er, Tsubasa Sato."

Don't mess up your own name, lady. Maou slumped in his seat.

"Oh. Well, my name's Maou."

"Maou?" The head under the newsboy cap tilted to the side a bit. Then:

"The king of the devils?"

Something in the pit of his stomach froze.

"Wha…?"

Maou was at a loss for words. Not a single human being had ever started a conversation with him like this. They made fun of him sometimes for how it sounded a bit like "devil king" in Japanese, but Maou made an effort to use a different intonation from that when stating his family name.

"Yes," Tsubasa Sato quizzically continued, taking Maou's hesitation as a denial, "like what final boss is called in the video games…"

"Not *that*," Maou replied, exhaling deeply. That intonation must not have come across to her. Tsubasa Sato sounded like a suitably Japanese name to him, but if she spent her childhood overseas up to now, that might explain her lack of practice with the language.

"Oh. Not a devil king, huh?" Tsubasa hung her head down. Apparently this came as a disappointment. But then she lifted it back up, suddenly realizing something. That cap over her forehead made it impossible to gauge her eyes, but there was a grin on her face.

"Oh! But, you know? My pop's name is Hiroshi Sato!"

"Huh?"

Maou took a look back at the father, wondering why this news was meant to be so monumental. The man lifted his head from his own book and met Maou's gaze.

"Hiroshi Sato, yes," he stated with a nod.

"Oh?" Maou said, a half smile on his face. He knew it was rude of him, but he just couldn't help it. The man wasn't exotically foreign—no blond hair or chiseled chin or anything—but his looks still indicated that "Hiroshi Sato" couldn't have been any less appropriate a name.

Ah, but it wasn't fair to have such preconceived notions about people, was it? Even if his face looked purely European to Maou, maybe he had some Japanese blood from his ancestors. Maybe his parents just liked Japan a lot. Or maybe he was a naturalized citizen who decided to adopt a Japan-style name. It was entirely possible.

"…"

They looked at each other for a moment or two longer before Hiroshi Sato averted his eyes, just like before. Maou couldn't guess what he was thinking.

Then the PA system sprang into action. *"Next stop, Test Site Front Gaaaaate, Test Site Front Gaaaaate. Disembark here for the Metropolitan Department of Motor Vehicles, Fuchu Test Center…"*

The ordeal was over. Maou was finally freed from this tragedy of a family. He reached out for the Stop button on a nearby safety rail. But then:

"Agh!"

Something pulled his hand back, keeping his finger away from the button by a few inches. Tsubasa had grabbed his arm again, and now:

"*...snif.*"

"What are you doing?!"

She was sniffing the back of Maou's hand, head close enough that she could almost kiss it.

"Tsubasa!" chided her father, face scrunched in frustration. Tsubasa, meanwhile, was inspecting Maou's hand closely, her face the pinnacle of earnestness.

"...I do not understand."

"That's what *I* wanna say!"

No point acting restrained now. He flung his arm away from her.

"What's with both of you guys?!"

If the genders were switched in this situation, it almost certainly would've been treated as a criminal matter by now. Maou wasn't interested in pushing the issue, but Tsubasa's behavior went far beyond what manners allowed on the bus.

"I do not know. The good scent is blocking it."

"Huhh?!"

"Maou's hand smells good."

What is she saying?

Maou was an earnest hand washer, a habit he had picked up from work. But today he had only done it once, after visiting the bathroom in the morning, washing with a cheap eighty-yen soap bar from the pharmacy that barely foamed up at all.

As this went on, the bus finally came to a halt at the stop in front of the Fuchu Test Center.

"Okay, um, bye!"

Tsubasa's bizarre behavior was concerning to Maou—but more than that, he just wanted to get away. He shot to his feet, headed past Tsubasa's side toward the front of the bus, and bailed out the door. The bus stop was across the street from the test site, so he half-jogged up the nearby pedestrian bridge and stormed past the front gate, praying he could file his papers before that wacky pair could exit the bus.

Hiroshi and Tsubasa wound up being the last out of the line of people exiting the bus. The fare from Chofu Station's north exit was 220 yen and they had to get change for a thousand-yen bill first. Predictably, it took a while.

"You must stop the standing out so much, Tsubasa," Hiroshi weakly warned.

"Aw, but this is first time!" Tsubasa replied, not at all cowed by this. "There is something with the man. His hand smelled."

"Smelled? ...*Gack! Koff koff...*"

Hiroshi gagged a bit at the exhaust from the bus as it rolled away.

"Yeah."

"It smelled how?"

"Hmm... I wonder where Maou is?" Tsubasa ignored the question as her eyes darted around the bus stop in search of Maou.

"...We need to take the test. I can pass it today."

"Good luck," Tsubasa blithely replied to her father's irresolute oath. After a few moments of fruitless searching, she joined Hiroshi up the stairs. "So, uh, this smell..."

"You do enjoy changing subjects, no?" Hiroshi marveled as he turned back toward the girl.

"You know what his hand was like?" she replied, ignoring him yet again, just as another bus arrived at the stop on the other side of the street. From above, they could see it eject another throng of test takers once the doors opened. Now Hiroshi had a hefty wait in line ahead before he could fill out the application. He sighed, expression unchanged, as Tsubasa prattled on.

"It smelled like oil, and potatoes, and...and something from long ago."

"Long ago?"

Hiroshi didn't know where the oil and potatoes came from, but Tsubasa's behavior indicated she found it important. She stood in place and, out of nowhere, began spinning around like a ballerina. Then, just as suddenly, she stopped, eyes turned toward the test site front gate.

"From long ago," she said in a low voice. "A place I was, long ago. A warm place."

❋

"Hey, do you smell something funny?"

Urushihara, seated at the computer desk, wrinkled his nose as he looked around the room.

"Bell's room," Ashiya replied, not bothering to take his eyes off whatever he was writing on the basic *kotatsu* heated table he was seated by.

Urushihara turned around. "Huh?"

What he smelled was something pungent, a sweet concoction that stimulated every nerve in his nose, like someone was burning or boiling a random assortment of herbs and spices.

"She is burning some kind of incense. She said she could use it to build an amplifier or something."

"...What's she doing in there?"

"I don't know. It still beats the pink smoke I saw seeping out from under her entryway yesterday. That came as quite the surprise, let me tell you. I suppose she's taking the kitchen-sink approach to her experiments."

"Well, if it comes out the windows," Urushihara said as he held his nose and turned to Suzuno's room, "isn't someone gonna report it as a fire or something? I mean, I guess she's searching for a way to figure out where Emilia is, but..."

"Who can say?" Ashiya listlessly replied as he continued taking a pencil to the paper on his table. Ever since the day of the scheduled birthday party for Chiho and Emi, Ashiya had been spending a lot of his free time writing like this. Urushihara figured he was doing some home accounting at first, but he was filling out five or so standard pieces of letter paper a day.

"You wanna borrow the computer?" he had offered once, in a rare fit of thoughtfulness.

"I don't know how to use it" came the blunt refusal.

This put Urushihara off enough that he vowed to ignore his behavior after that, but given that he began this habit right after everything that happened, he figured he was making a few Emilia-related efforts of his own. It was too extensive to be any standard sort of home bookkeeping.

But just then...

"Whoa!"

"Mgh?!"

The apartment shook a little.

There was an impact from Suzuno's room, one large enough to safely term an explosion. Both of them yelped in surprise.

"Ooooh...*koff koff*..."

From out their open window, they heard Suzuno opening up her own window and coughing out of it.

Urushihara and Ashiya exchanged a glance for a moment. Then they both leaned out the window, dodging the morning's laundry hanging out to dry right now, and tried to gain a better look.

"Whoa! Dude, what're you doing in there? What's with all that smoke?"

Suzuno had pushed the window fully open in order to escape from what were now billowing clouds of white smoke from her room. She held her face out as far as she could, tearing up as she coughed.

"L-Lucifer... I apologize...*koff koff*...but I think I failed the incantation a little..."

"If failing it means you're gonna level the apartment, could you do it outside, dude?"

"N-no," came the raspy reply. "I had gone around old antique shops for items that might serve as amplifiers, but the spiritual corpus instilled within them all clashed with each other... *Koff koff koff!*"

Urushihara shook his head in exasperation. Ashiya took his position at the window.

"What is the meaning of this, Bell? Because this is *not* very neighborly behavior, I don't think! What if all our clothes start smelling like whatever it is you're brewing in there?"

Even as he griped at this, he was rapidly plucking laundry off the lines outside. Devil's Castle was slightly downwind from Suzuno's room at the moment. She, meanwhile, was taking deep breaths outside, most of her weight now placed on the window frame.

"This, this should not be terribly difficult as long as I have access to the right tools… Here I am, declaring myself Chiho's 'instructor,' and just look at this pathetic display…"

Although it was nowhere near the level of Chiho's, Suzuno's own morale had clearly flagged over the past two weeks.

"So, not too much progress yet?"

"No, sad to say," Suzuno said, breathing a sigh of relief as the mystery smoke finally dissipated.

"Look," Ashiya shouted as he moved the laundry over to the other window, "I don't know what you're doing in there, but please ventilate your room a little more before cooking again. It will be the end of us all if you start a fire in there."

Suzuno, still draped over the window frame like a comforter hung out to dry, weakly waved a hand. "I just wish," she moaned, "there was someone on Ente Isla we could trust apart from Emeralda and Albert…"

"If there were," Ashiya spat back, "would you have to go through these ridiculous incantations of yours?"

Silence met the accusation. Suzuno knew full well he was right. "So be it," she said. "I will wait a while, then try another approach… after I clean my room."

Just imagining the state of her room right now made them shudder. Between the smoke, explosions, and general state of clutter, it couldn't have been the neatly organized space it used to be.

"Apart from Emeralda, huh?" Urushihara pondered for a bit. "Hey, Bell?"

"Mm? What?"

Urushihara didn't respond immediately, still fumbling with something in his mind. After a moment, he took out a piece of paper, about the size of a business card. It was hard to say where he got it, considering he almost never left Devil's Castle—and with all the scuffs and folds on it, it was in pretty poor condition.

"Outside of Emeralda and Albert," he said as he looked at the slip of paper, "I don't know about who you can trust, really…but I can think of someone who'd know about something if you asked—"

"Ahh!!"

Before Urushihara could finish, there was a shout from the road beneath both of their windows.

"Hm?"

"Ah!"

"…Who's that?"

The person they saw by the side of the apartment was looking up at them, waving, a mixture of surprise and joy on her face—although Ashiya and Suzuno could sense the anxiety behind the smile.

"Hello, Ashiya. Hi, Suzuno… Umm, I guess this is the first time we've met, but you're Urushihara, yeah?"

Urushihara raised an eyebrow, not expecting this unfamiliar woman to know his name. "Um, who are you, dude?"

"Ms. Suzuki…" Ashiya murmured.

"Rika, what are you…?"

Neither he nor Suzuno could hide their surprise at the sight of Rika Suzuki looking up at them.

"A little tea?"

"Oh, thanks," Rika replied at Ashiya's offering. They had let her into Devil's Castle, and although she spent her first few seconds there studiously observing the space, there wasn't all that much to observe, really. After that, she simply stared at the tabletop in the center of the room, politely waiting for Ashiya to sit down first.

"I need to thank you again for helping me with the television earlier," Suzuno said. She had changed to a new kimono before entering Devil's Castle.

"But I am impressed," Ashiya added as he sat on the tatami-mat floor, "you managed to discover the address."

"Oh, uh, I exchanged addresses with Suzuno over our phones when she bought the TV."

Suzuno blinked and pointed at herself. "With me?"

"Y'know you can put a lot more than just your name and phone number in your contact list, right? It kinda depends on the model, but with a lot of 'em, you can use an infrared link to exchange all that info in a flash."

"Ah." Suzuno nodded with a warm smile, recalling how they had done just that at the electronics shop. Rika guided her through it herself. "Well, superb, then. I had nothing private written on mine, and it brought you here safely, at least."

"Yeah. Kinda funny how you wrote 'inquisitor' of something or other in your job description, though. I don't think I've even heard of that word before."

The smile froze in place.

"...Ha-ha... Is that what I wrote?"

"Yep."

Rika seemed neither suspicious of Suzuno nor interested in carrying the subject any further, but Suzuno awkwardly averted her eyes anyway. Urushihara glared at her, silently gloating at her stupidity.

"Nngh..."

Thankfully, Rika gave her no time to wallow in self-pity at her mistake.

"So, uh, I thought it'd be bad of me to just stop by without contacting you or anything, but I kinda felt like I had to do *something*, so..."

The usually bright expression Rika wore was now dour, clouded. Ashiya could already guess what she was going to say.

"...I dunno if I'm barking up the wrong tree, but...have any of you guys heard from Emi lately?"

He was right.

Emi mentioned she had requested a little time off from work for her little trip to Ente Isla. But *little* was the operative word. She was supposed to be gone for only a week. And now Emi had been AWOL from her job for two weeks straight.

"I mean, she's not answering her phone or responding to my texts. I got up the nerve to visit her apartment, but she wasn't there...and she hasn't reported to work in a pretty long time now."

"So did they f...er, what kind of footing is Yusa at workwise at the moment?"

They hadn't known each other for that long, but Ashiya could tell nonetheless that Rika's apparent serenity was just a front. He strained to avoid stressing her out too much.

"They're still kind of tolerating it for now...but, like, she's never been late to work once before this, and all her evaluations have been superexcellent up to now, so the floor chief and manager and stuff are really a lot more worried than angry, I guess you could say."

"I see..."

"But Emi lives by herself, right? And her parents are overseas?"

"In-indeed..."

Ashiya paused for a moment, unsure if he should be agreeing to this. They had never bothered comparing notes on their respective improvised backstories.

"It didn't seem like she had a whole bunch of friends outside of work, so I'm just worried that... You know, if she got sick or had an accident, maybe no one would have any idea at all, so..."

"..."

Now Rika's eyes were pointed at the floor. Ashiya took that opportunity to give both Suzuno and Urushihara a furtive glance. This long with no contact would make near anyone fear the worst. The glance, before he turned his eyes back to Rika, was his way of telling them that the optimist's scenario wasn't going to work here.

"So when I tried thinking about Emi's friends that I knew, Maou and you guys were about all I could think of, so... I'm sorry I'm butting in and all, but I couldn't just sit there any longer..."

Neither Ashiya nor Urushihara were socially backward enough to correct Rika on the "friend" bit. But they also knew that neither of them would be much help to her at the moment.

"Sad to say, Ms. Suzuki…but none of us know any more than you do."

Rika did not show much in the way of disappointment at this. She was no doubt prepared for it—or it might be more accurate to say that she wasn't expecting much more than that from them.

"Do you know why Yusa took off from work in the first place?"

"Indeed," Suzuno said, "it was something to do with her family. She did not seem to wish to discuss it much, so I avoided asking where she was going, exactly…"

If it were Maki Shimizu, their other mutual friend at work, she might've had the gumption to ask Emi point-blank about her family roots. But to Rika, subjects like that were practically taboo in her mind. The vast earthquake she experienced as a young child growing up in Kobe had something to do with that, but even without that past, an adult woman talking about having to handle "family issues" was always a topic best dealt with carefully.

"Yes," Ashiya added. "That is all I know as well. I heard she was returning to her family home, but as for where that is… Well, to be honest, I had little interest in that question at the time."

He was straining himself now, keeping the lies as little and insignificant as possible to keep himself secure.

"You neither, Suzuno?" Rika asked, hoping for perhaps something different from a fellow woman.

But all she could do was parrot Ashiya. "I apologize… I know of nothing else."

One couldn't blame her. Rika would never believe the truth. It would just throw her into even more of a panic.

"Yeah… I guess not. I'm sorry I had to barge in here and bring all this stuff up out of nowhere…"

"…Are you doing all right?"

They could all tell that she was straining herself. Ashiya was genuinely concerned that Rika would fall over at any moment. But she didn't, although her posture wasn't what it used to be.

"I just… I mean, what could've happened to her?"

Rika was talking for everyone in the room. Nobody added to it. A heavy silence loomed over the apartment.

"You think maybe we should talk to the police about this?"

"Dude, wait a sec…"

It was Urushihara who found himself reacting to Rika's completely sensible suggestion. Everyone else knew that this was nothing the Japanese authorities could do much about, but now *he* had gone and reflexively said it.

"Yeah," Rika said as she turned to him and shrugged. "Like, maybe we're friends, but we're not related or anything, so I kinda feel awkward about getting the cops involved and making this into some big thing…but then I think, oh, what if something happens to her while we're hemming and hawing about it, y'know?"

"Rika…"

Although a little relieved that Rika took Urushihara's reaction as simple reluctance, Suzuno couldn't help but feel for her plight. She reached out to pat her on the shoulder.

"Still, though…"

But before she could, Rika's next words changed the entire atmosphere of the room.

"I mean, totally falling out of contact for an entire week? That's just weird. And that's one thing, but not even going back home, either?"

"Huuuh?"

All three of them gasped at once.

"…What?"

"Ms. Suzuki?"

"Yeah?"

"…What did you say just now?" Ashiya asked, eyes round and wide.

"Just now…? Um, like how it's weird she's not back at home?"

"No, dude, *before* that! How long's she been out of contact?!"

"Huh? Like I said, about a week ago…"

This was starting to agitate Rika a little. It was agitating the other three quite a bit more.

"Now…now wait just a moment, Rika. Are you sure about that? Quite sure?"

"Wh-what do you mean?"

"I mean, when was the last time you spoke with Emili—with Emi?"

"Um, last Friday night, but…?"

"Last Friday night?!"

Now it was surprise that ruled over Devil's Castle. Last Friday night would have been one week after Emi was supposed to return home. It had been two weeks since Maou or Suzuno had any idea where she was, and yet she made contact with Rika a whole week after that?

"Um, why're you acting so surprised about it?"

"We, we've been out of contact with Emi since Friday two weeks ago. *Three* weeks, actually. She was supposed to return home on that Friday, and nothing since then."

"Huh?"

"Did she contact you by phone, or text?"

A text, Suzuno reasoned, could easily have been sent by an impostor. But Rika quickly foiled that thought.

"It was over the phone."

"And, and you're sure it was Emi?!"

"Umm, hang on a minute…"

The sudden energy from the other three in the room unnerved Rika a little, but she nonetheless took a mobile phone out of the bag she had along and brought up the call-history screen.

"I think this was the call from Emi, but…"

But, for some reason, the entry Rika pointed out had "Number unknown" written on it.

"The number was unlisted?"

"Wow, and you don't block calls like that?"

"I have no idea why, but my family's landline's set up to block caller ID by default. My granddad uses that phone to call me up sometimes, so…"

"But if the number was blocked," Suzuno said, doubting the

evidence presented to her, "perhaps it was someone disguised as Emi, no?"

"Ooh, I doubt it," Rika rebuked. "It was definitely her voice. She identified herself as Emi before I could say anything, and, like, it was just a normal conversation between us. I mean, I work for a phone company, so I'd think I'd spot it if it was a scammer or something."

"*They're* the ones you gotta watch out for, dude..."

Urushihara's under-the-breath whisper went unnoticed.

"What did you talk about?"

"Um, nothing too much. Just about our shifts and stuff... Oh, and I just remembered. You said Friday two weeks ago, right? She called me up on that Friday, too."

Rika tapped at her phone again, then showed the screen to Ashiya. Another call from an unlisted number.

"I remember she asked me if we could trade shifts the following week—so, like, last week's shifts."

"The following week? I thought Yusa was working practically every day of the week."

"Nah, I think she was reducing her workload a bit this month. I'm pretty sure she was only scheduled for three days on that week. And, um..."

Rika suddenly looked at Ashiya. Their eyes met, and much to Ashiya's puzzlement, it made Rika look a bit panicked.

"Well, you know, I'm not exactly a social butterfly, either, and there were a few shifts I wanted to get that week but couldn't, so I said okay to it. Kinda worked out for both of us, y'know?"

Ashiya and Suzuno exchanged glances. As far as they could tell, there was no reason to doubt Rika. If they were talking about things like that, the idea of an impostor seemed unlikely. And there was nothing about the calls that indicated Emi was endangered, or even perturbed. But something did stick out.

"And that was really it, huh?" Urushihara questioned. "Nothing unusual about it?"

"Hmm?" Rika crossed her arms, deep in thought. "Well, I dunno.

Not really. Emi ain't really the type of girl to talk on the phone very long. I can't think of anything out of the ordinary."

"So you were talking about work shifts in both calls? That was it?"

"Huh? Well, yeah, I think so. The second call was pretty much just a thank-you for taking her shifts."

Rika didn't sound too concerned about the content of the calls. To the rest of them, it created new issues to tackle. What were Emi's intentions—what kind of situation was she in—that she felt compelled to make these perfectly normal phone calls to her coworker? She must have known that going incommunicado for a week past their planned date would freak Chiho and Suzuno out—and on that first week, all she decided to do was thank Rika for a workplace favor?

It was a bombshell on what had otherwise been a dead end for the demons. They knew they couldn't let this clue go unexplored.

"All right," Suzuno began, "so you did not talk about anything besides work shifts? About the weather, perhaps? Or did she greet you differently from usual? Anything!"

The sheer force behind the question made Rika dig into her memories one more time, bringing a hand to her forehead. "Boy," she said, "you hear that question a lot in dramas and stuff, but I never thought someone'd be asking me that."

A few moments of silence, and then:

"Hmmmm, well, here's the whole order of the first call. I get a call from an unlisted number, I pick it up 'cause I figure it's my family, and it was Emi. She was talking kinda fast… Like, not really waiting for me to respond, y'know? And it sounded like her voice was kinda far away, too. She said her parents were overseas, so, y'know, I figure she was just tryin' to end the call fast so she didn't pick up a ton of roaming charges or whatever."

The words came in fits and starts as Rika continued to probe her memory.

"The connection sounded pretty unsteady, too. Like she was calling from a basement or something. She must've been out in the country or someplace pretty far from a cell tower, I figure."

It would be pretty far, yes. Another planet, in fact. But the three of them nodded silently at her, nobody wanting to interrupt her train of thought.

"Oh! And there was something or other on a PA system behind her. Like, really loud. That's why I figured she wasn't in Japan anymore."

"Broadcast?"

"Yeah. Uh, I dunno what language it was, but… Y'know how they broadcast the *bon-odori* dance music at superhigh volume during summer festivals and stuff? It sounded a little like that. So then, uh, she was talking about swapping shifts and then, ooh, I think, uh…"

Rika interrupted herself to take a notebook out of her bag, flipping through the pages.

"Oh, here it is. There was one day out of the ones she talked about that I wasn't sure I could cover. So I was like, 'Hey, I think Maki's free'—oh, she's another girl we know at work—'I think Maki's free, why don't you ask her?' And, oh, actually, that was kinda odd, too, now that I think about it…"

As Rika put it, here was how Emi responded to the suggestion:

"She said she couldn't call Maki for some reason. I thought, well, that's weird, 'cause I knew she had her number and everything. But then I realized I never called her, either—we just texted each other, 'cause we're on the same network. So maybe not, y'know? So I wound up volunteering for that day anyways, and then she was, like, 'Okay, thanks' and she hung up. So then, last week's call, uh… That was just, like, 'Thanks for taking the shifts.' But there was something playing behind her then, too. We still just talked about work shifts, though."

What could that mean?

There was no telling what that background noise could be. But if the call had come from Ente Isla, then why was she calling Rika, of all people, about work shifts, of all things? One would think she'd sound more urgent, at least, if she was in actual trouble—but why were they having a nice, leisurely chat about work instead?

And that wasn't even the biggest question.

"Why Rika, though…?"

"Huh?"

"Oh, er, sorry," Suzuno said, covering for her unintentional whisper. Not to be rude, she thought, but if Emi's life was in danger, calling Rika would do little to change that—something Emi had to know herself.

Something *unexpected* had happened to her. That much was certain, at least. It wasn't something that directly threatened Emi, but it still meant she couldn't return home on time, so she asked Rika to pick up a few shifts in the meantime. Was that it?

"I doubt it."

Emi was safe enough that she could chitchat about work shifts with Rika, but she contacted only Rika. There had to be a good reason for that.

"…Ah, one moment."

It was Ashiya who broke the silence brought on by this torrent of information.

"Shut the windows, Urushihara. We have rain."

"Huh? Oh, yeah."

"Well, look at this," Suzuno marveled. "I thought the forecast said it would begin in the afternoon. Oh, dear, my window is still wide open…"

It was still sunny when they first spotted Rika on the road, but now the sky was gray and depressed, droplets of rain falling from it. Suzuno hurried out to shut the windows she had flung open before nearly dying of asphyxiation.

"Oh, don't you have laundry hanging out there?"

Rika stood up, spotting the laundry Ashiya had just moved from the window closest to Suzuno's room.

"M-my apologies," Ashiya blurted out. Towels, socks, and a few pairs of boxers with the elastic all stretched out were right in front of them—not the sort of things a man wants hanging around while entertaining the opposite sex.

"Ah, it's all right!" Rika smiled as Ashiya frantically tried to take the clothes down. "I'm not some spoiled little rich girl who gets all hot 'n' bothered over a coupla undies hangin' in the air, y'know?" Then her own face grayed as she looked out the window. "Whoa, it's gettin' pretty dark over there. They didn't call for that much rain, did they?"

Ashiya, with laundry hangers in both hands, looked in the same direction. "It could be quite the storm, yes," he said. "Not to eject you from our place, Ms. Suzuki, but do you have an umbrella?"

"Yeah, just a little travel one...but you mind if I wait it out in here for a little bit? I wanna talk a little more about what each of us knows about Emi, and plus..."

Squinting out the window, they could see that, not a terrible distance away, a virtual cascade of rain was even now advancing upon Villa Rosa Sasazuka.

"I don't think a travel umbrella's gonna help much against *that*, y'know?"

Before Ashiya could nod his agreement, they heard thunder from outside, the sky suddenly darkening with it.

Suzuno chose that moment, with a couple of clangs and thumps, to rush in from the adjacent room. Her phone was in her hand, the screen lit up. She had apparently received a message.

"This is an emergency!"

"Wh-what?" Rika's stared wide-eyed at the near-frantic Suzuno. She didn't answer her, instead giving Ashiya and Urushihara glances.

"Lucifer!"

Right after calling him that in front of Rika, she tossed something at Urushihara with her free hand.

"...Dude, is this one of those bottles?"

It was a bottle of 5-Holy Energy β—an energy drink that also served as Emi and Suzuno's lifeline on Earth, the only way they had to recharge their holy force.

"We just received an SOS from Chiho!"

"Huh?"

"From Ms. Sasaki?"

"Chiho? Y'mean *that* Chiho?"

Not willing to spare a single moment, Suzuno thrust the phone's screen at Ashiya and Urushihara. "Unlisted," it said. The two demons looked at each other. This was no normal SOS. It was a true emergency, transmitted via Idea Link.

"Lucifer, you are the only one right now. We must fly off immediately. It was from Chiho's school!"

"Chiho Sasaki's school…? Uh, Sasahata North High?"

Suzuno, in so many words, was recruiting Urushihara to join her as backup if it was needed. Normally, whether Chiho was involved or not, Urushihara would reply to this with an "*ugggh*" and a quick trip to his closet. Now, though, his face was oddly resolute. He stood up—and that, more than anything else, shocked Ashiya. He was going out? To help Chiho? At his enemy's request? *In the rain?!*

"H-hold on!" Ashiya bellowed, trying to make Suzuno remember Rika was here. "Kamazuki, what is going on? Calm yourself!"

"We haven't a moment to lose. If Chiho is telling the truth, there is a chance she, the school, and the entire neighborhood are in mortal danger. I apologize, Rika, but I must explain this later."

She and Urushihara exchanged a nod before they each chugged their respective 5-Holy Energy βs, as if starring in the latest TV ad campaign.

❋

"Hey, what the hell?"

Maou winced at the window. It wasn't looking too nice outside.

According to his watch, it was just past eleven in the morning. He heard rain was in the cards for today, but nothing like this giant storm cloud—and not this early, either.

"Probably shoulda known I couldn't count on the forecasters when rain gets involved…"

Whining at Japan's meteorologists about forces of nature wasn't too constructive, he knew—but to a Devil King that, at his peak, could conjure and manipulate the very atmosphere around him, he really wished the perky weather girl on the local morning news would work a little less on her makeup and more on actual science.

"...Wish time would go a little faster," he mumbled as he watched raindrops beat against the window.

Despite the difficulties he had concentrating earlier, he was absolutely sure he was comfortably within passing range this time around. Once the list of passing applicants showed up on the electronic board in the waiting room, he was expecting to hit the track outside for the on-the-road exam. But:

"This ain't gonna happen, is it?"

The rain outside was accompanied by what seemed like typhoon-class winds. He had hoped for a little rain, actually, polishing his dedication to safety in adverse conditions. He'd need those skills for the job. But would the DMV officials let him out there in weather like this? Nobody had announced anything yet, and it would still take an hour or so for them to grade the tests and announce the results. It was hard to say whether the rain would be gone by then, but considering the guerrilla rainstorms that petered out within an hour in mid-August, maybe he had a chance after all.

Either way, it meant that all he could do now was sit around the waiting room and watch the rain fall. He had a lot of company among the other applicants, at least, each one taking their positions on the bare seats and reading books or playing with their phones as they awaited the fateful moment.

Maou was among them, sitting on the far end of a long bench, but his phone was a Stone Age relic capable of voice, texting, and nothing else. He never adopted the now-common habit of staring at his phone when there was nothing else to do, and he had never purchased anything as lavish as a paperback book before in his life. Most of what Devil's Castle retained were either borrowings from the library or cookbooks Ashiya picked up from the used-book shop.

"Maybe we're stayin' healthy," Maou mused to himself, "but culturally, we're almost totally shut off from society, huh?"

Most of his time in Japan so far had been spent working. It might be about time for him to try to gain a broader perspective of what Japan was all about. This driving test, along with the MgRonald Barista seminar he attended a while ago, was providing him with some sorely needed inspiration. In Japan, there wasn't a single thing he couldn't study if he wanted to. Taking a systematic approach at some institution of higher learning would be a fair ways off, but considering how his company was covering some of the testing costs for him now, he already knew there were ways even a low-class wage slave like him could gain some support for it.

Even more, it was starting to seem fun.

"...Maybe I oughta hit a bookstore on the way home. I've got some spending money."

Whenever he didn't use the three hundred yen Ashiya gave him daily for "food costs," he always kept it in his private stash. He had some free cash to work with out of his own paychecks, too, but Maou considered that more of an emergency fund for unforeseen disasters.

More to the point, if he had a license to drive, that would make so much more of Japan suddenly available to him. The idea of having room to roam, without being reliant on public transportation, seemed revolutionary. He would have to actually obtain his own cut-rate scooter first, but as long as he wasn't picky, Maou figured he wouldn't have to wait too long.

"Lot more to dream of, I guess."

The smile on his face was quite unsuited for the outdoor weather as he pondered over the possibilities. But then, a dark shadow crossed it.

"Heeeeyy! Maou!"

"......Yeah?"

It was Tsubasa Sato. He didn't need to raise his head to make sure. Of *course* they'd met again—they were all trundled to the same waiting room after the exams. And when he did look up, he saw the girl in the newsboy cap again, fluorescent lights illuminating her from behind. Hiroshi Sato, her father, was standing a little bit away.

"...How'd the test go?"

He didn't know whether Tsubasa took a test at all, but he asked anyway.

Hiroshi heaved a sigh befitting of his stature and general atmosphere.

"I think I maybe failed it."

"Nooo! Don't *say* that!"

"Half the problems...I could not read."

"Um..." Maou felt obliged to comment on this little dialogue. "Look, don't you think you should give it a rest for a little while? You're wasting a lot of money on testing fees."

Assuming Tsubasa wasn't just feeding Maou a line—Maou wasn't too sure—this was the tenth straight exam, which meant he had paid out for it ten times. A scooter license was one thing, but for a full-on automobile license, the costs must have been insane.

"Do you have a license from your home nation, Mr. Sato? Maybe you could just get an international driver's license or something."

"No."

"...Oh."

He would've appreciated a little more effort to keep the conversation going.

"Where Pop is from, there are no cars at all!"

"Huh?" Maou asked.

"Tsubasa!"

"Oh, sorry, sorreeee!"

Maou cocked an eyebrow for a moment as Hiroshi admonished his daughter for some unseen affront or other, while Tsubasa showed zero remorse at all. He didn't bother dwelling on it for long.

"But, ah, you are right," she continued. "It is waste of money."

"Well, I don't want to pick on Mr. Sato or anything, but—"

"I said I can read problems for him, too..."

Maou chuckled. "I don't know why you can read Japanese when your father can't, but you have to take the test yourself, all right? It'd be cheating if you read the questions for him. You might even get arrested."

"Cheating? You mean, something…sinister?"

"I'm impressed you know that word, but…yeah."

"Oh, why bother with the license, Pop?"

It sounded a little impertinent of her, but even Maou had to agree. It beat flushing money down the toilet like this. "Yeah," he said, "I know it'd be useful to have, but there're probably a lot of better ways to use that money."

"Yeah, Pop! Forget about license. Just drive wherever you want to any—*mmph*!"

Maou didn't know how serious she was, but he covered her mouth with a hand anyway. Making bold declarations like these inside the local licensing agency was far too dangerous. Luckily, there was a wall on one side and a man listening to loud music from his headphones on the other.

"Mmph?"

"Look, you realize we're in a government office, right?"

"…"

Maou removed his hand. "You can't have someone read the problems for you, and if you start staying crazy stuff like that, they might ban you from having a license in the first place. Be a little more careful, all right?"

"Ohhh. But what is problem if nobody catches us—*mmmph*!"

"I told you, you can't say stuff like that!"

"…I think he is right, Tsubasa."

"Could you try and make her put a lid on it more often, sir?" said Maou, fed up at the spring of tepid reactions from the man.

"Mpph mph!"

Tsubasa, whether she was listening to Maou or not, started waving her arms around. Maou removed his hand again. Her rapid-fire bombshells and overly friendly demeanor made him do it, although he now realized that he kind of overdid it with a strange girl he had only just met. *Good thing Chiho and Emi aren't here*, he thought to himself. The thought came up pretty often in his life.

"..."

Just as he was about to sit down on the bench, mind still in a muddle:

"...Hey."

Tsubasa grabbed the wrist of the hand Maou had covered her mouth with, stopping him just as he was about to reach the seat.

"Snif snif..."

Yet again. Why was she so obsessed with his hand?

"Yeah... Something behind the potatoes...*snif.*"

"Look, what are you—?"

"*...lick.*"

"Agghh?!"

Now even the guy in the headphones was staring at Maou. With the noise he just made, it'd be odder if he didn't. She had just licked the palm of his hand.

"Wh-what the hell're you doing?!"

This was the most bizarre ethical dilemma Maou had ever encountered during his time in Japan. It made him glow red with shame.

"Did you...just now...?"

Maou made the pointless gesture of holding his battered, moistened hand behind him as he babbled at her. Tsubasa paid him no mind, newsboy cap still covering most of her head as she pondered over something.

"Hmmm..."

Then she nodded, apparently reaching her conclusion.

"Pop, I think this man is it."

"Hmm?" Hiroshi said, surprised at this new conversational path.

"Can I take off hat, Pop?"

"...Do not do the standing out too much."

They were already standing out far too much for Maou's tastes. But after receiving Hiroshi's permission, Tsubasa nodded to herself, deftly took a hand up to the brim of her cap, and:

"...!!"

The face revealed under it made Maou forget to breathe for a moment. Not just the face, either. The hair under the cap, and the

lazy-looking eyes staring up at him, both threw him for a total loop. Her face was attractive and well proportioned, but it had a languid expression on it, like her mind was occupied with nothing at all. She was probably a little younger than Chiho.

But that wasn't the problem. The real issue was her purple eyes. And her hair was silver, long at the sides and cut short behind them. Even under the dim fluorescent lighting, it still shone a bright, eye-opening color.

And beyond all that…

"…Wait, are you…? That hair…?"

"Hmm…"

Tsubasa twirled her side hair around a finger. There was a whorl of purple to it. It nailed Maou to the spot, reducing him to broken sentences.

For her part, Tsubasa blithely nodded.

"I thought…from smell, maybe it was you?"

"The smell…?"

Maou recalled the handful of times she had gotten a whiff of his hand.

"I don't know you, but my nose is right." She rubbed her nose proudly with a single finger, smiled, and laid another salvo upon the foundering Demon King. "You know my sister Alas Ramus, yes, Maou?"

"……………………………………………………………………………Huh?"

This had already been flustering enough for Maou, but what Tsubasa just said sounded even stranger to him.

"Sister?"

"Uh-huh."

"Um…?"

"Sister. Alas Ramus, I mean."

"…Huuuh?"

There were a few things Maou needed to tell this pair. He knew there had to be. *What's with the hair? Are you two really father and daughter? You aren't from Earth, much less Japan, are you? If you look like that and know Alas Ramus's name, you must be born from a Sephirah, right? What have I got to do with you?* And while he had them here, he needed to interrogate them about their lives in Japan and get their names, addresses, phone numbers, and maybe their IDs, too.

But beyond all those practicalities, there was something Maou absolutely had to get straight first.

"You mean…sisters by blood?"

"Uh-huh. If it is same Alas Ramus, Maou, she's my elder sister."

There couldn't have possibly been many more children out there with the singularly inconvenient name Alas Ramus. If Tsubasa already knew it, there was no point dwelling on the question. But something else bothered him even more.

"If you're saying she's your *elder* sister, does that mean…you have that kind of close familial relation going on?"

"Close familial…what?"

"…Wait."

Suddenly, Hiroshi—or whatever his real name was…the person provisionally being called Hiroshi—laid a heavy hand on Maou's shoulder.

"I think…what you think, it is probably correct."

"Could you explain a little more what you're so positive about, please?"

All Maou was trying to do was figure out what *sister* meant here. To him, the question drove at the very creation myths that described how Earth and Ente Isla began. It made his head swim.

"Um… Her sister?"

"Agh, you guys are a pain to talk to!" Maou was about ready to pitch a fit. "Okay, let's try it another way! Sir, I want you to be quiet for a moment or two, all right? Now, Tsubasa."

"Uh-huh?"

"Are you saying," Maou said, choosing his words carefully, "you're Alas Ramus's *younger* sister?"

"Uh-huh!" She brightly nodded.

"…Why?"

Tsubasa's bodily structure, the silver hair with the purple whorl, was exactly the same as Alas Ramus—the telltale sign of a Sephirah-spawned creation. It couldn't have been some fashion thing; not if she knew the term "Alas Ramus."

Still…

"Hey! Don't look! I know I am pretty!"

Tsubasa smiled as she chided Maou. He was currently scoping her out from head to toe.

"…I *so* want to hit you."

Even in this era of equal rights between genders, Maou thought he was justified. He still somehow managed to bottle up his anger in the end.

As Maou reckoned earlier, Tsubasa was a bit younger—and certainly more childlike—than Chiho. But to put it another way, she looked like she was in middle school. Why would she call a toddler like Alas Ramus her elder sister? There was no way of telling how they grew and matured, certainly, considering their otherworldly origins. One grew more rapidly than the other, for reasons Maou couldn't fathom—but this rapidly?

There was no doubting now, at least, that they were involved with Ente Isla.

Maou took a look around, then whispered into Hiroshi's ear.

"You're both from Ente Isla, aren't you?"

Hiroshi's eyes opened wide in surprise, unexpectedly. "How… Who are you…?!"

"You got a girl like *this* with you and you think nobody would notice?!"

Dealing with Hiroshi was starting to tire Maou out. He stood back up from the bench and motioned for the two of them to follow along. It wasn't anything he didn't want others to hear, but he didn't want to be considered a weirdo, either (although it might've been too late for that).

They took position toward the service windows at the front of the building, shuttered now that testing was done for the day. A number of people walked to and fro through it, but none of them were interested in stopping to eavesdrop on random strangers. The only open window was on the other side, for people looking to renew their license.

"Right. First off, can I have your real names? Both of you."

Tsubasa and Hiroshi exchanged glances with each other. *Must be having trouble figuring out who I am*, he thought.

Then Hiroshi's accent started sounding greatly different. Or, to be more exact, his choice of language.

<"It might be strange to ask for confirmation at this point, but we have no indication that you are not our enemy yet. You know that we have come from Ente Isla, a world completely different from this one. Who *are* you?">

Both Hiroshi's speech and manner of presenting himself were now a far cry from the sluggish demeanor of the past. Maou didn't detect any holy force within him, but between his eyes and his language skills, he knew he was more than just another middle-aged man.

<"...Common Vezian, is it?"> Maou said, matching his tongue. <"From the eastern part of the Western Island?">

Apart from Holy Vezian, the language of choice on the westernmost section of that island—the part the Devil King had never managed to conquer—Maou didn't need any demonic force to make himself understood in any language on Ente Isla.

<"Sorry,"> he continued, <"but lemme ask the questions first. I had thought I knew about everyone who came from Ente Isla or elsewhere. I want to know where you come from. Besides, you might be the first clue I've had yet.">

<"Clue?">

Maou nodded and turned to Tsubasa. <"I was too surprised earlier to ask you, but I think I better right now. Were you born from a Yesod fragment?">

That, to him, seemed worth confirming first, before moving on to her "sister." Maou could hardly contain his excitement at having this gift from Ente Isla appear out of nowhere for him. But Tsubasa's reply was light and airy as always.

“Yes! I surely am!”

And she gave it in Japanese, too.

“Pop, you are sure you will say everything?”

“…” Hiroshi was still suspicious of Maou’s motives. Tsubasa apparently took that as her “go” sign.

“Well, okay, Pop. I think it is okay. Maou isn’t an ‘angel.’ I see that, too.”

She rubbed Hiroshi’s arm in an attempt to quell his fears, her purple eyes aimed right at Maou.

“My name is Acieth Alla. ‘Tsubasa,’ it is a fake name.”

Acieth Alla. Maou took a deep breath at the name, oxygen flowing through every vessel in his body.

<“‘Alla’…? Wing? Is that why you went with Tsubasa? The same word in Japanese?”>

“Uh-huh! I like sound of it!”

Maou simply nodded. <“So you and Acieth aren’t connected by blood, right? You made up that Sato name, too, didn’t you?”>

The idea of Hiroshi being his real name seemed ludicrous by now. He had to have another one, just as the Devil King Satan had the name Sadao Maou.

<“I took the name Sato from…a man I encountered, not long after I arrived in Japan.”>

<“Just a normal Japanese guy? You didn’t reveal who you were, did you?”>

Hiroshi (provisional name) shook his head. <“No. He was a strong, gifted man, and so kind to me despite my total lack of knowledge about Japan. No matter how many times I fell, I picked myself up and kept aiming for my dreams. I did whatever work I was offered. It was fun to me, every day.”>

Maou didn’t ask how hard it was for him. He wasn’t stupid enough to, because he knew that he himself was the main and most direct reason for all this.

<“You boarded the carriage from the observatory. Have you been living in Mitaka this whole time?”>

<"No. We were near Shinjuku at first, but we moved to Mitaka because Sato heard what Tsubasa...what Acieth dreamed of, and he made some introductions for us.">

Maou groaned. They could have run into each other at any moment. For that matter, it wouldn't have surprised him if they had picked up on Maou's and Emi's activities to some extent by now.

<"...Okay, so I don't know your real name, but I think I might know the names of some of the people you're involved with.">

"Why is...talking like the merry-go-round like that?"

There was no telling how much longer Tsubasa—or Acieth Alla—was going to continue indifferently commenting on their conversation.

Then Maou realized something. <"Hang on. You can't speak Common Vezian?">

"Uh-uh. But I understand it! Like this..." Acieth pointed at her temple, then Maou's forehead.

<"An Idea Link? Wait, so *you* can't use it, though?"> he asked the man.

<"Regrettably, I have neither the knowledge nor the talent required to cast magic. It has...not been easy for me,"> Hiroshi stated.

Maou nodded. Hence the literacy issues, he supposed.

<"So, these people you say you might be familiar with...?"> Hiroshi asked.

<"Yeah..."> Maou fixed his gaze on Hiroshi again. <"But if I'm going to reveal it, I want to be sure you're willing to work with me. I'll help you and Acieth out as much as I can, too. So don't run away on me, all right?">

Hiroshi's eyebrows lowered. <"I am not a child, either. Given the Common Vezian we are speaking, I hardly expect we can be strangers now. But you, as well—if you're willing to go this far, you had best not do anything to oppose me. I am worthless with magic, but I think I am capable of defending myself well enough.">

Maou noticed Hiroshi turning his eyes toward Acieth as he spoke. He opted against bringing it up. <"Well, you said it. I'm just saying, I don't want you chickening out on me.">

He paused a moment, grinning, before coming out with it.

<"My allies and I are searching for Emilia Justina. She had been located here in Japan, but she returned to Ente Isla several weeks ago and we've lost contact with her since. Do you know anything about—">

"Emilia?!"

The reaction was dramatic. The bold, defiant glare Hiroshi had been aiming at Maou up to now dissolved in an instant. The moment the name "Emilia" came up, it was like all of the blood immediately rushed up into his head.

With his two long, powerful arms, Hiroshi placed his hands on both of Maou's shoulders. He brought his face up close to him, excited to the point of nearly hyperventilating.

<"Y-you know Emilia?! Do you know where Emilia is right now?! H-how could she possibly be in Japan?!">

The voice was deep and booming enough to make passersby stop and give him strange looks. Hiroshi was in no position to care about them.

<"Calm down! Stop shouting like that! You'll attract attention!">

<"How...how can I calm down at a time like this?! Where is she?! Where is Emilia?!">

"I told you, calm down!" Maou said, finding himself reverting to Japanese as he waved his hands at Hiroshi.

<"Come on already!">

<"...All right. Listen to me. Emilia was definitely in Japan, all right? But certain things happened a few weeks ago that drove her to go back to Ente Isla for a bit.">

<"Are you...kidding me?">

<"But it's now been two weeks since the date she said she'd return. We're not capable of traveling to Ente Isla to look for her. It's a long story. That's why you're the only lead we have right now on where she is. A complete stroke of luck!">

"Luck? How rude!"

Hiroshi, ignoring Acieth, staggered over to the shuttered reception window, leaning against it before gradually dragging his body downward to the floor.

"Hey!" Maou extended a hand to support his arm, not wanting Hiroshi's emotions to draw the attention of someone important. "Don't make this any harder on us, all right?"

<"Emilia... Emilia's...">

"Great... So you know Emi, huh? I should've known, I guess..."

If Acieth was cut from the same cloth as Alas Ramus, that meant they were both linked by their Yesod connection. Perhaps with Emi's holy sword, too. But this wasn't the sort of reaction an involved party would make if they were aware of Maou's and Emi's activities over the past year or so. It must've been the case for Acieth as well.

And it gave Maou the inspiration to go back over all of his and Emi's relations—all of the Hero's and Devil King's—over the past few months. His brain powered into overdrive, and before another moment elapsed, it arrived at a conclusion.

"Hang on, are you Emi's... Emilia's...?"

<"Emilia... Emilia is my daughter... My precious daughter!">

<"...Oh.">

"Pop's real name is Nord. Nord Jus...Jus... Um, what was it?"

Acieth's uninvited aside provided Maou all the confirmation he needed. So there they both were—Nord Justina, Emi's father, and Acieth Alla, child of the Yesod Sephirah. It was a completely unexpected piece of luck. *There's no way I can let this pair disappear on me*, Maou thought.

"Hmm?"

Then the mobile phone in his pocket started ringing. He couldn't think of anyone who'd need to call him at this time of the day. Probably Ashiya, he supposed, using Urushihara's computer to call him and find out whether he passed the test or not. Maou had much bigger fish to fry right now—two of them, in fact—and it couldn't have possibly been anything more important. He decided to ignore it and interrogate the man in front of him while he had the chance.

He didn't receive it.

"Pick up the phone *now*, you stupid Devil King!!"

"Wagh!"

"Aiggh?!"

The screamed command thundered across Maou's mind like a sledgehammer. He nearly lost consciousness for a moment, but he still had the mental strength to take his phone out of his pocket. It was from an unlisted number—and before he could even push the "OK" button, the shouting came back.

"Devil King! I know I'm connecting to you. Answer me right now*!"*

"Wha… Suzuno?! What's with you all of a sudden?"

It was definitely Suzuno's voice, brought vividly to his mind via Idea Link.

"This is your *fault for not picking up! This is an emergency! Come back to Sasazuka as soon as you possibly can!"*

"Huuuh? Come back? What're you…?"

Maou looked up at the two people in front of him. Nord, Hiroshi no longer, was sitting in a shattered heap on the ground. Acieth was staring goggle-eyed at Maou for some reason, in a state of total surprise over something or other.

"I'm kind of busy right now, okay?" Maou pleaded, bringing the phone to his ear—an unnecessary step for him, but one he made to avoid suspicion. "I still haven't gotten my license yet, so it's not like I can just wheel back home right now…"

But Suzuno wasn't listening. She had reason not to.

"We received an SOS from Chiho!"

"What?!"

"Devil King! Is it raining where you are?!"

"Y-yeah, it's comin' down like a typhoon out there…"

"It's centered right over Sasazuka! This typhoon-level storm descended into Tokyo from out of nowhere, and it's blowing wind and rain all across the city! And it's parked over Sasazuka…right on top of Chiho's school!"

"Wh-what the hell?!"

This was crazy, and he had no idea what any of it meant. But there was no reason for Suzuno to lie about it. And, as if to back up her story, the building's PA system squawked to life.

"Um, this is a notice to everyone inside the testing center. We are about ready to announce the results of the motor scooter licensing examination, but due to inclement weather, we will need to delay the start of the on-road exam. Please consult one of our staff at the test registration window for more details. All applicants renewing their automobile licenses should also—"

"A typhoon? That's ridiculous..."

"Whether it is an angel, demon, or human, I cannot say, but someone is using today's bad weather to deploy a massive incantation over the city! You need to come back here, now! I don't know how long Lucifer and I can hold out! It is right over Chiho's school!"

Then, having said her fill, Suzuno shut off the Idea Link.

Maou grabbed his head. "What in the hell, man? I—I can't just run home now! I still got these guys to deal with!"

If Chiho was in danger, he wasn't about to weigh that against the fate of his test score. But even if he shot out the door right now, he had a bus and a train to ride before he reached Sasazuka. It'd easily take an hour or so. Even if he shelled out for a taxi, the driver couldn't go too quickly in *this* weather. And above everything else, he couldn't simply abandon these two golden opportunities that just dropped in his lap.

I knew I should've kept some of the demonic force I gave back to Farfarello!

It had taken Maou a month to realize that, but it was approximately one month after he could do anything about it. He never imagined that Emi, by far the strongest out of them all, would disappear on him.

"...Guess it's taxi or nothing!"

It was the only practical method to bring these two with him to Sasazuka. The potential fare waiting at the end physically pained him. He'd have to put it on the card and worry about the details later.

"Hey, uh, Maou?"

"What?!"

"Are you in the hurry, or something?" Acieth gingerly asked.

"Yeah, but I don't even know what I should be doing right now. It's driving me nuts!"

"That woman's voice, it came from Idea Link, no?"

Maou eyes shot open. "You heard that just now?"

"Uh-huh! More or less."

There wasn't any "more or less" about it. But she was right. Maou recalled how Suzuno's initial bellowing startled her as well.

"So what do you do? Because if you go now, that is not good for us."

"Well, yeah, me too! If I could, I'd take you two with me and teleport our asses back to Sasazuka right now!"

"Sasazuka?"

"Yes! The neighborhood I live in! Goddammit! If I could still fly, I could get directly over there, too!"

He didn't have much idea how much distance was involved as the crow flies, but a Devil King flying at full speed would probably reach Sasazuka in pretty short order. Besides, although he was too flustered to remember it right now, Satan also had the ability to open Gates whenever he wanted.

"So you want all of us to fly?"

"Yeah, and I *can't*, all right?!"

"Me, Maou, and Pop, yes?"

"Yes! Look, we don't have time to talk. I need to catch a taxi… And will you stop feeling sorry for yourself down there? Get up! We're both gonna have to ditch the test again!"

Maou was trying to work the haggard Nord back to his feet when:

"*Huff!*"

He suddenly floated. Physically. Into the air. Inside the test center.

"Hey, *whoaahh*!!" Maou shouted, flailing in order to reach the ground again. But before he could:

"Maou, Pop, *huff*!"

Acieth gave them both a look, then lifted her body into the air, just like Ashiya in demon form.

"A-Acieth! We're being too conspicuous! Way too conspicuous!"

They surely were. Three human beings, up in the air—physically, and emotionally to boot. Acieth ignored the chatting around them as she used her mind to pull Maou and Nord close to her, float out into the torrential downpour, and then soar into the dark, cloudy skies.

"Aaaaaagghh?!"

The sheer speed of their ascent made Maou scream out loud. Acieth paid it no mind. He could tell she was using some kind of telekinetic power to free them from the bonds of gravity, but since there was no magical barrier or other protection, he and Nord were rapidly soaked by the rain surrounding them.

"Maou, which way?!"

"Which what?! I have no idea where we are!"

"That lady, she said it was the weather magic, yes? It must be *there*!"

"Whoooooaaaaahhhh!!"

Before Maou could even gauge the geography beneath him, Acieth shot off toward the eastern skies, not bothering to keep either of them upright in the process.

"We need hurry, yes? Let's go!"

"W-wait a sec! I need to get my body—*gaaahhhh*!!"

"Here we goooooooooo!!"

"......"

Accompanied by Maou's scream and Nord's voiceless groan, the three of them set off from the Fuchu Test Center eastward to points unknown.

THE DEVIL IS A
LITTLE LATE TO
THE PUNCH

Ashiya was at an impasse.

The eyes Rika Suzuki used to stare at him, as she knelt politely on her side of the low table, felt sharper than the edge of the Better Half blade. He had never dueled directly with Emi's sword, but if anything, he would have preferred that sight before him right now. That, at least, could be countered with physical force.

"Ashiya, why aren't you saying anything to me?"

"I...um..."

He was once called a tactical genius. Now, kneeling at a table, Ashiya was incapable of coherent speech.

They were alone in Devil's Castle. The tatami-mat floor was starting to dampen a bit along the edge facing the backyard. Rika was rotating her gaze between the rear window and Ashiya.

Between them, sitting on the table, were two small, empty bottles.

"I'm asking you to tell me."

"Uhmm, I-I completely understand what you wish to say, but..."

"Y'know, I always thought there was something a little mysterious about you, but I didn't think we, we were, um...close enough that I could start to get all nosy and stuff, so..."

Despite stumbling a bit midway, Rika's voice remained sharp, probing.

"When you bought that TV, too, I just figured, like, 'Ahh, I could ask him some other time,' but...you know."

"Y-yes..."

The rain outside had lowered the temperature considerably, but he could tell that his back was drenched in sweat.

"And, if you don't mind me being honest with you right now, I have absolutely no idea what's going on."

"I...I suppose not, no..."

All Ashiya could do was crack a smile, one even damper and more sorry looking than the half-dry laundry piled on the floor.

"So I'm gonna ask you one more time."

"Y-yes?"

"Where did Suzuno and Urushihara just run off to?!"

She was no longer phrasing it as a question. It was an order.

"And in this rain, too!"

A finger shot toward the window.

"They jumped right out of there!"

"Nnnh..."

Ashiya was solidly against the ropes.

Just as Suzuno came back to Devil's Castle upon closing the windows in her room, she received a phone call. It was from Chiho, and while he would've guessed Chiho would seek Maou's aid first, attempting to complete an Idea Link from Sasazuka all the way to Chofu was probably too long a distance for her to grapple with quite yet.

But did all of this have to happen right now? At this very moment? With *her* along for the ride?

It had been just over a month since Chiho gained her Idea Link skill. She had just used it for the very first time.

Two weeks on from Emi's unexplained disappearance, they all knew inside that this was worthy of being termed an emergency. One where every second potentially counted. But why did Suzuno and Urushihara have to act that way? Chugging their energy drinks, tossing them on the Devil's Castle floor, then:

"Let's go. Stay close to me."

"Sure thing, dude."

They opened the window right before Rika's eyes. What were they thinking?

"W-wait, you two! Stay calm for a..."

"Hey, what're you guys doing? You're gonna...?!"

Ashiya and Rika both tried to stop them, albeit for differing reasons. But as the two of them unhesitantingly opened the window and plunged down into the hurricane-force storm:

"Huh?"

They didn't plunge from the second floor at all. They flew horizontally forward before alighting on the roof of the building across the street.

"Wha...what?"

Rika, eyes open wide, couldn't help but open her mouth. Behind her, Ashiya's head was deep within his hands.

They must have flown up there to confirm where the threat came from. Suzuno pointed in a seemingly random direction, and with that, the two of them began bounding from roof to roof, making superhuman leaps into the air as they disappeared into the storm.

"Ah...?!"

"Ah...!!"

The look on Rika's face when she turned to Ashiya was like nothing of this world. She had been, in her own way, a great help to him, and among human beings, he enjoyed her company nearly as much as he enjoyed Chiho's. That was what made her face at that moment—eyes filled with shock, suspicion, and a longing for some kind of explanation—such a trauma for him to behold.

So Ashiya found himself kneeling at the tale, writhing under Rika's stare from the other side, for approximately fifteen minutes after the other two left.

"Rrgh..."

"Hm?!"

Rika's eyes dug deeper into him. He would be provided with no attorney, no right to remain silent. He knew Rika wouldn't be willing to accept any of this without some kind of justification.

But he wasn't just giving her the silent treatment. He honestly had no idea how much he needed to explain to her. Rika wasn't part of the human-being contingent of the Devil's Castle regulars. She was Emi's friend, and he could tell from their past interactions that Emi had revealed nothing to her. If Ashiya decided to lay out all of Emi's secrets now, he couldn't imagine what kind of drama that would wreak upon her return. At the same time, he didn't have enough of the demonic power he'd require to erase Rika's memory later on, nor any way to replenish it—not like Urushihara, who apparently received his demonic (holy?) strength out of a bottle.

They were supposed to be comparing notes about Emi's disappearance. Why'd it have to turn into *this*? In a corner of his mind, he complained to himself about how talentless he was proving to be.

"Well…it's like this."

"Yes?!"

"Kamazuki, you see…and Urushihara, as well…"

"Uh-huh?!"

"They were doing…focus-group testing, for these energy drinks…"

"And?!"

"I suppose…those are the results?"

"Caffeine doesn't make you do *that*!!"

Rika slammed a fist on the table. The bottles wobbled in the center as Ashiya's back shot straight into attention.

"I mean, when Red Buck says it'll give you wings, they don't mean it literally!"

She stood up and stormed toward the window.

"From here, to the house over there, it's got to be at least thirty feet! You can't jump that far without even a running start! If you could, you oughta be competing in the Olympics!"

"Y-yes, I know…"

"…Look, Ashiya. I'm not trying to accuse Urushihara and Suzuno of being space aliens or supermutants or anything."

Ashiya was sure Rika was picturing something close to that in her mind, but there was no point saying that.

"But even if this was some kinda Hollywood stunt with wires or whatever, you could still tell a little that it's fake! But they did that all by themselves! Who are they, anyway?!"

There, at that very moment, Ashiya discovered a glimmer of hope. Rika was preoccupied solely with Suzuno's and Urushihara's apparent superhuman skills. It would do little more than buy him some more time, but maybe he could put the blame on *their* shoulders and play dumb about the whole thing! Would that work? It wasn't much to cling to, but it gave Ashiya a little hope.

"And you saw them go off without acting one single bit surprised! You were just trying to stop them or whatever! That can't be the first time you've seen something like that from them!"

Curse the women of Japan! So sharp-eyed and observant! Even in his current pit of despair, Ashiya felt deeply astonished. Astonished, and back at an impasse again.

"...If I could be honest, Ms. Suzuki, I have my doubts whether you would believe me or not..."

Ashiya sighed and resigned himself to his fate. He had never formulated some grandiose scheme to actively hide his true identity, and besides, it was Suzuno who caused all this anyway. Who could admonish Ashiya for being forced to reveal everything in circumstances like these? They all would once they found out, yes, but...

"...I'm not a stupid enough woman that I wouldn't believe what I saw with my own eyes, Ashiya."

Perhaps recognizing his imminent defeat, Rika sheathed her verbal sword and sat back at the table.

"And I think I'm...kinda prepared for the worst, y'know?"

"The worst?"

"Yeah. What you told me before, about how you ran a company with Maou... That wasn't a lie, but it wasn't really true either, was it?"

"...What makes you think that?" Ashiya asked, eyes squinted nearly shut.

Rika shrugged. "Oh, I dunno. I just kinda thought it. Like, when you were picking a phone after you bought that TV. You said normally, you and Suzuno shouldn't be getting along at all, right?"

"Yes, I...think I might have said something of the sort, perhaps..."

"But when you were talking about Suzuno upstairs at Sentucky Fried Chicken that first time, it sounded like you actually really cared about her, right? Maybe you never got along with Emi, but at least with Suzuno, you treated her like an actual neighbor and stuff. But you didn't know her at all before she moved next to you, right?"

"Um..."

"'Cause if not, why did you say you *shouldn't* be getting along? Two neighbors who hated each other's guts wouldn't go on shopping trips together, and it's like... I dunno. Like, maybe you didn't realize it, but you actually knew each other a long time ago, or maybe you just knew about each other before now. And I'm guessing that's how it is with her and Emi, too."

"Ms. Yusa?"

"Yeah. 'Cause, like, nowadays, Emi treats Suzuno totally different from when I saw her at the office for the first time. At first, she was so cautious around her that I thought maybe she had worked for Maou or something in the past. Nowadays, though... They get along so well, I'm a little jealous, even."

Now, alongside his continued astonishment, Ashiya was cursing himself for all the little mistakes and giveaways they had made.

He didn't know when Emi had discovered Suzuno's true colors, but at the time of their little Sentucky outing, Suzuno was nothing more to him than a girl living next door who had just given them an enormous box of udon noodles. Any care he had betrayed for her at the time wasn't an act, really, but once he learned the truth, he inadvertently went off script. He *knew* he should've kept up the façade of neighborliness around Rika, but he hadn't. And Rika wasn't a dull enough woman that she let that inconsistency escape her.

"And even before then, I thought you guys kinda had a lot of stuff between yourselves that I didn't have a window into, but it wasn't until that shopping trip when I started thinking there was something y'all were keeping from the world. Like, between Suzuno, and Emi, and... Well, I know we only just met, but considering that circus act just now, probably Urushihara too, huh? So what was that, anyway?"

"..." Ashiya steeled himself. He had mentally prepared for this eventuality long ago. If it meant Rika would be too terrorized to come near them any longer, that was simply destiny playing its hand. Part of him figured that she wouldn't try selling the story to the media. They had not known each other that long, but on that score, at least, he was confident.

"Ms. Suzuki."

"...!"

"So. All of us...are—"

"Eep?!"

"?"

All that resolve, all that resignation that drove Ashiya to expose himself, was extinguished by Rika's short scream. She was pointing a shaky finger at the window Urushihara and Suzuno had flown out of. He turned around, following it...

"Agh!!"

...and let out a yelp of his own. He couldn't help it, considering what was there.

"Ashiyaaa...open uhhppp...open da window..."

It was a sopping-wet, semiconscious Maou tapping at the window.

"H'loooo... Ashiyaaaa..."

He was the very definition of the word *pitiful* as he tapped away, plastered against the wall like a drowned rat instead of being out in Fuchu passing his road test.

Overcoming the first wave of surprise, Ashiya hurriedly rushed to the window and flung it open. It was definitely Maou on the other side—but what flew inside along with the wind and rain was something else entirely.

"M-my liege?! What are you doing out there?! And who are these people?!"

"Nnhh... I'm freezing... Uhh, I'll explain later. Lemme get this guy down. Ngh..."

Instead of entering the room, he kicked a large, just-as-soaked middle-aged man inside. He lifted his head up from the tatami-mat floor.

"...Who's this?"

"I-indeed..."

Neither Rika nor Ashiya had ever seen him before.

"Oh... Rika Suzuki? You're here? Well, umm... I'm kind of in a hurry, so let's talk later... Ashiya, can you get this guy in a new set of clothes for me? He says he's got battle experience, but right now, we can't afford to let him go free."

"My, my liege, what is the meaning of—"

"L-later, all right? Sorry. Suzuno's gonna freak if we're delayed any more. I guess Chiho's in trouble...eh-*choo*!"

"Ah! Huh? It's only been fifteen or so minutes since Ms. Sasaki contacted us..."

Maou couldn't have predicted all of this in advance, Ashiya thought, and there was no way he could've covered the distance from Fuchu in such a short time.

"May I, too, come out, Maou?"

"Sure, go ahead. Oooh, it's cold..."

They turned toward the unfamiliar voice, only to find an unknown woman who was quite literally and unabashedly floating in the air. Ashiya turned to Rika, only to find her eyes darting rapidly between him, Maou, the woman, and the middle-aged man.

"Your Demonic Highness! This girl...!"

"Oh, once I'm at my destination, I'll make her come back here, too—"

"Okay, here we go!"

"I'll explain laterrrrrrrrrrrrrr..."

Before he could finish, the two of them left the waterlogged man behind and flew off the way Suzuno and Urushihara had. It took a few moments for Maou's shouting to fade into the distance.

Ashiya and Rika watched them go, completely forgetting to close the window behind them for a moment.

"......"

"......"

"......"

"Well...um. Do you have, ah, the clothing?"

"Who in the blazes *are* you, sir?!"

"Did she just flyyyyyy?!"

It would be a while before order reigned once more.

⁂

Just a bit before Maou received Suzuno's Idea Link call:

When she saw him, walking carefree across the school courtyard in the pouring rain, Chiho almost fainted on the spot. Not out of horror—just out of the sheer suddenness of it. It probably should have paralyzed her in fear, but she had already met one of their kind face-to-face (although that one had looked just a bit different). And after everything she'd heard about them, she knew that this guy must've been fairly high up among the demons in Ente Isla. One of the bosses, the leaders of the Malebranche tribe.

That one who had Erone with him… Farfarello! That was the name. He was one of the new guys, it sounded like, but from far away, the Malebranche stalking school grounds right now looked a decent amount larger.

She was too shocked at first to notice, but he was dragging something along in his right hand. She realized it was *Peace and Truth*, a sculpture donated by alumni to commemorate the fiftieth anniversary of the school's opening. The design was bizarrely abstract—a sphere with geometrical patterns on it, surrounded by three naked men with their backs arched, arms open wide. Ever since it was installed on school grounds, students treated it with equal parts disdain, discomfort, and denial of its artistic qualities. Now it had been either uprooted or snapped off its base by the Malebranche, who was cheerfully walking around the courtyard as the sphere dug into the soil behind him.

Not long ago, she had made Maou and the others worry for her thanks to an overhasty decision. But, likewise, she knew she couldn't handle this alone, so she tried to contact Maou. He had mentioned that he was going off for his retest today, but this was probably more important.

But she couldn't reach him. Avoiding the students and teachers currently awestruck at the sight of the Malebranche, she had focused on her cell phone with all her might, yet failed to link up with Maou at all. Not even this amplifier was enough to reach Chofu, she inferred.

She knew that Emi was still missing, and that meant the only one of them capable of taking on that demon in combat was Suzuno. While the attention of everyone else in the classroom was focused on the courtyard, she grasped the phone inside her bag once more and attempted an Idea Link to her. This time, it worked, with Suzuno promising to rush over as quickly as possible.

"Hey, Sasachi, what do you think that is?" blurted out Kaori Shoji, her best friend at school, as she pointed at the courtyard. Chiho wasn't about to explain to her.

"Um… Boy, who knows? Hope it's not a rabid zoo animal or anything…"

She silently apologized to the demons of the world. And while it couldn't have been in response to that, the Malebranche roughly tossed away *Peace and Truth* like a baby growing sick of their toy.

Chiho, and everyone else, gasped as the work of art hurtled its way to a corner of the courtyard like a meteor, smashed against one of the soccer goalposts, and shattered. If they had been less lucky, it could've hit the school building itself.

"Maybe I could do something for…a little bit?" Chiho said to herself. Divert his attention, for example. Maybe she could make the Malebranche move away, to someplace where students wouldn't see him. She grabbed at the phone, seeking Suzuno's opinion, but realized that Suzuno would never want her acting on her own. It was probably better to sit back and observe how things unfolded, Chiho reasoned to herself—

"Grooooorrrrrrrrhhhhhhhhh!!"

"Aahh!"

The Malebranche roared, its loud howl echoing high like a wolf in the wilderness. Chiho reflexively covered her ears.

"Ah…"

Then she heard someone gasping in fear nearby.

"Y-you okay?"

"I think we better run away…"

"What should we do, teacher?"

"What? D-don't ask me…"

The classroom was starting to fall apart. Chiho had the vague feeling this was how the seeds of panic unfolded. She looked at the Malebranche, still far away, and came to a conclusion inside her mind. Maou and Suzuno might yell at her later, but there was no time for indecision. If the Malebranche outside did something like that again, that'd just add fuel to the flames of panic.

"..."

Chiho slipped out of the anxious classroom and sprinted down the hall before anyone noticed. It was probably the first time she'd run down a school hallway at full speed since kindergarten.

Soon, without anyone noticing, Chiho was on her way to the rooftop of the old Sasahata North school building. The school had been in operation for over seventy years, and the older building was past half a century old. Renovation plans didn't look like they'd come to fruition during Chiho's time at the school, but apart from the classrooms for the third-year students, the building was chiefly used for meeting rooms, student-council facilities, and other activities that didn't involve hanging out there all day.

Everyone was too focused on the horror at hand to notice Chiho as she flung herself into the old building, now empty as she sped down the hall and up to the roof. But just before she reached it:

"...Ah?!"

She stopped.

Right next to the third-floor stairway—the only way to the rooftop—was a classroom the students commonly called the "forbidden chamber." Not that a student died or got locked up in there or anything; it was once the home-ec classroom, but now there was one in the comparatively spiffier, thirty-year-old "new" school building, so it had merely fallen into disuse.

There was a padlock on the door, but the fitting it hung from was flimsy enough that a child with a screwdriver could've pried it open. Chiho had gone here earlier to "witness" Emi making the leap between worlds through her Yesod fragment, but now she could see that someone had bashed in the forbidden chamber's door from the inside. The hallway was also plastered with comically large, muddy footprints.

"...He came in from there?"

Chiho peeked inside the chamber. There was no sign of damage—just some old desks, sinks, and bookshelves with thick layers of dust on them. But she could see brand-new burn marks in the middle of the floor. What could *that* be?

"...Oh, now's not the time for this!"

She could go in-depth on it once Suzuno arrived. The Malebranche outside came first. Running up the stairs, Chiho was met with a door that was obviously going to be locked. But this wasn't a problem for her. She looked around the rest of the floor, ensuring nobody was around, then took a deep breath.

"Welcome to a new morrrrrniiiiing!! A morning filled with hope for aaaaaaall!!"

Focusing on the powers deep within her, she began belting out the song from the morning radio calisthenics program, activating her holy force. There was no need to go this far for Idea Link purposes—but she wasn't activating it to cast any other sort of spell, either. She knew from her training that the longer she sang, the more power she could activate—so she sang it over and over, extracting all the holy force she could.

At around the third repetition, her efforts paid off. She could feel some kind of large mass arrive at the other side of the door.

"...Did you call for me?"

It was a quiet, heavy voice, similar to Farfarello's. Chiho breathed a sigh of relief. He must have picked up on the holy energy she was releasing.

"...Well, good thing you can speak Japanese."

"Who are you? Why did you summon me?"

"Um, it's kind of a lot to explain all at once...but I just thought we could talk a bit, before the other students and teachers tried anything dumb against you."

"Hmph," the presence disdainfully grumbled. *"Bold words, considering the pathetic amount of holy force you wield."*

Chiho, fortunately, was mature enough to admit when someone was right, no matter how scornfully he put it. "Well," she responded, "I really don't have the power to fight or anything, and I don't think

I could do anything against you anyway. But I called you here for a really good reason."

"Oh?"

None of this was scaring Chiho all that much—partly because this presence was unseen, partly because she was sure Suzuno was nearly at the school by now.

"Could you open this door for me with your strength? I couldn't bring a key up here with me. You Malebranche can do that much, right?"

"..."

The sense of indecision on the other side of the door was palpable.

"You see, they're pretty rough on children in this world. If I asked a grown-up to borrow the roof key so I could talk one-on-one with a demon from another world, they probably wouldn't give it to me."

The moment she fell quiet, the heavy steel doorknob began to rattle.

"...!"

Then she could hear it be crushed on the other side. Just as she thought, he had broken down the lock for her. The knob, losing its mounting, fell to the floor by Chiho's feet.

The hole it created was occupied by a single, sharp claw, one that looked familiar to her. *That* scared her—Farfarello didn't do much to faze her, thanks to the way he relied on Erone for most things, but now, she was about to go face-to-face with a demon she knew nothing about.

It'll be all right, Chiho said to herself as she watched the door creak open. *These demons... You can talk things out with them, it turns out.*

"Huh. You've got guts, don't you, you puny little excuse for a human girl?"

The voice was rougher, more uncivilized than Farfarello's; a good match for his much larger size. The claws weren't as long as she had thought at first—he had a large body, but the claws and wings and such were actually a bit more compact than the other Malebranche she had met. But the sheer demonic force exuding from him was a far cry from Farfarello's. It wasn't Maou-as–Devil King level, but without having unleashed her own full holy powers beforehand, just standing next to him would sicken her enough to keep her from even speaking.

"You appear to be a human from this nation…but judging by the way you stand before me without faltering… Hmm. You are the one that little minnow Farlo has prattled at me about? The so-called MgRonald barista, general in the New Devil King's Army?"

Being asked deadpan by an officer-class demon from another world about her workplace qualifications almost made Chiho laugh. And was "Farlo" the nickname they had for Farfarello over there? It was kinda cute.

"I suppose there's no need for an introduction," Chiho said, attempting to give him a bold smile instead of ruining the atmosphere. "Hopefully you will be just as polite and gentlemanly as the other demon I met before."

The large demon roared in deafening laughter, blowing his fetid breath around the area as he did.

"Gah-hah-hah-hah-hah!! You should know your position in the world, girl. Your voice is shaking. You cannot hide your fear of demons!"

"Ah…!"

Chiho reddened at the presence of this unknown threat.

"But though a rotten ant you may be, you are a rotten ant with guts. If it is human politeness you seek, then allow me to introduce myself first."

"S-sure…"

Chiho took a look at the sky behind the Malebranche's back. Suzuno still wasn't there.

"You may call me Libicocco—as you no doubt inferred, one of the chiefs of the Malebranche. But know this, girl: I am not a toddler among men, like that pipsqueak Farlo. While I rejoice at the news that our lord the Devil King is alive and well, I refuse to accept the appointment of this new set of four generals!"

The wind and rain suddenly strengthened. It wasn't her imagination playing tricks on her. The faraway clouds began to darken and bunch up against each other, visibly in motion as they descended upon the cityscape. The power of this Malebranche, Libicocco, was now too much to fully dispel with her activated holy force. That was the main reason why not even Chiho was willing to correct him and mention there were now *five* generals.

❋

"Ah—agghh!!"

Suddenly freed from the bonds of Acieth's telekinesis, Maou fell on his rear end, straight onto the wet ground.

"Come on, man! What's with you? We aren't at Chi's school yet!"

"Sorry. A little side trip."

The rainwater had now thoroughly soaked him down to his underpants. He looked down at his legs, resigned to his fate.

"...Damn, this is seriously a major typhoon... Hey, why're we at MgRonald?"

Looking up, he realized he was in familiar surroundings—the MgRonald in front of Hatagaya rail station. At least this weather kept anyone from being near them. That was a relief. He couldn't see how Kisaki and the crew were holding up since they didn't land (more like drop) within eyeshot of the registers, but scoping out the tables, he could tell the rain wasn't exactly making customers swarm over.

"Even if we put up those banners, they'd probably be ripped apart by now, huh?"

They had turned the vertical banners advertising their new fall campaign sideways, following company storm guidelines, but the weights holding them were still clattering in the wind.

"Someone was...here, no?"

"Huh?"

Acieth was looking nowhere near the MgRonald. She was turned toward Sentucky Fried Chicken across the path. Maou followed her eyes to the rival chain.

"...Whoa! They all right in there?"

One of the large windows overlooking the dining area had been shattered to tiny bits. The wind must've driven a rock or something through it. Maou hoped that none of the crew or customers were injured, although he couldn't have cared less about the archangel managing the place. It looked like the lights were out as well—maybe a lightning strike had triggered the circuit breakers.

"But...he not there anymore."

"What? You got something to do with SFC?"

Perhaps it was a given that Acieth Alla, being so similar in nature to Alas Ramus, would spot the presence of the archangel Sariel. But what did she mean, "not there anymore"?

"...I'm sorry. You are in hurry. No more delay."

"Nnnh.........!!"

Before Maou could reply, Acieth violently cast him into the air. Just as she did, the two of them disappeared into the sky, sucked up by the rainclouds.

❋

"So, Libby-cocka, what brought you here to Japan...or to Earth, for that matter?"

The howling wind and rain had soaked both her school uniform and her hair. The demon's huge body and huger magical force unnerved her. Both considerations were making Chiho shiver at the moment as she attempted to push the conversation forward. It didn't look like he had any Erone-style backup at his side, but there was no telling yet. She recalled the vast army Ciriatto had taken with him to Choshi.

But Libicocco scowled in reply, a scowl that, even to someone relatively new with demon body language like Chiho, made it clear he was in a foul mood.

"The way you pronounce your words truly annoys me."

"Huh?!"

She was trying to figure out what the demon wanted—only to have her diction criticized?

"It is Libicocco. *Say it again."*

"...L-Libi-cocka?"

As demonic conversations in the pouring rain go, it was generally dissatisfying for both sides. But Chiho kept up with the impromptu language lesson, not wanting to fall further on his bad side.

"'Cocka'? Do you want to die? I am not a rooster."

"Oh, do they go cock-a-doodle-doo on Ente Isla, too?"

"Are you making fun of me? Allow me to give you a word of advice: If you mispronounced names like Draghignazzo or Scarmiglione in front of them, they'd have your head off, human. They are young. Hot-headed. Very intolerant of mistakes."

"Do...du, Dra...Drag-nihh... Oh, geeeeez."

This was too much to handle. Chiho didn't know much about popular demon-baby names in this day and age, but assuming Malebranche were named by their parents, it seemed like giving them such unpronounceable names was like making them go through life with one hand tied behind their back.

"Well, no matter. Just remember that much for us. The rest are gone anyway."

"Oh?"

Something about this casually thrown-out statement sounded important to Chiho. But in the next instant, Libicocco's voice bellowed out again:

"One more time! Libicocco!"

"Li... Libi-cocco!"

"Fine! See? You could do it the whole time! Not quite native-level, but fair enough for a human from another world. I will allow it."

"Th-thanks..."

At least she passed *that* test.

"So, Li...Lib...Libicocco, what is it that brings you here...?"

"I'm here to kick some ass."

"Huh?"

Chiho thought she had messed up his name again, inspiring more ire. But it didn't seem to be that.

"When I say that, however, I do not mean grand massacres or anything of the sort. I am here in this set of buildings because that is where the Gate took me. I was merely told that I should bash things up and cause as conspicuous a disturbance as possible, wherever I found myself."

"As...conspicuous?"

"Yes. Like this."

With a gnarled grin that exposed rows of pointy fangs, Libicocco summoned a mighty wind as he raised his arms into the air. Chiho covered her eyes with a hand as the rain and wind surrounding Sasahata North High School seemed to compress and whirl within itself, like the school was now in the eye of a major hurricane.

"W-wait! Stop that!" Chiho shouted.

The storm on the other side of the border was like nothing before. It was a violent wall of rain and wind, sending roof tiles flying from the surrounding houses, knocking over garden trees, and slicing live power lines in half.

"*See?*" Libicocco crowed as he cast his meteorological magic, gauging Chiho's reaction as he did. *"Conspicuous, is it not? Perhaps I should try this next."*

His clawed fingers danced in the air around him. Chiho couldn't tell what had changed. But then she felt the hairs on her nape stand up, and then light flashed across a calm, soundless world.

"Aaaah!"

Chiho's scream ripped through the air. It seemed like the wall of rain had set off the light, but then she noticed the countless bolts of lightning that now crashed down from the heavens. They touched down one after another on roof antennas, on telephone poles, and on lightning rods perched over apartment buildings. But their sheer number, enough to make one's vision fully white, had to be too much for the town to handle.

"Hmph. This isn't working."

The lights stopped. Chiho carefully opened her eyes, then gasped as she noticed several buildings around the school now on fire. Not even that was enough to satisfy Libicocco.

"Bah. I was hoping that would generate more of a sea of flame."

Chiho was expecting exactly that after such an onslaught of electricity. But with all the precision electronics in modern homes, a lot more thought had been given to lightning protection than in previous generations. Electric lines hung on poles were also more heavily protected than before, since they were now being used for Internet connectivity and a host of other applications; lightning-safe equipment was a legal requirement in all electrical facilities now. The effect of all those wires and poles acting as electrical grounds meant that Libicocco's anticipated firestorm never came to pass.

But that didn't mean he was done. Far from it.

"Well, I suppose it needs a little more power, then."

Of course he would do that.

"Wait a minute, please! What's the point of doing all this?!"

"Huh?"

"Just spreading chaos like this…? The demons who came here before had an actual purpose. Whether it was getting Satan back or taking Yusa's…taking the Hero Emilia's sword away from her, or whatever. Is this all you want to do?!"

"Rather talkative ant, aren't you?"

"Libicocco, your mission is light-years more low class than what 'that pipsqueak Farlo' was doing! Why don't you act more like the arch-demon you are and do your evil with a little more class?!"

"Girl, do you have the wrong idea about this?"

"…What?"

"Right now you, the kids in this facility, and everyone else in the neighborhood are being struck by fear. They're racked by feelings of horror and sadness. I don't know what kind of grand mission that little rat Farlo betrayed to you…" He grinned. *"But a job like this is what every demon dreams of! Spreading terror and desperation provides us with a feast of demonic power!"*

Once again, Libicocco spread his arms out, straining them even more this time.

"Ohh…!"

Exposed to the emanating demonic force, Chiho found it hard to breathe. She fell to her knees. Activating all her holy force at once drained it far too quickly. *Time for a 5-Holy Energy β*, she thought—but her spare bottle was still inside her schoolbag. She couldn't show her back to Libicocco now—this demon was cruel enough to snuff her right out if she did.

"If you don't like it, you're free to stop me by force," Libicocco scoffed, as Chiho felt her strength wane. *"You* are *the MgRonald Barista, our next great general and leader...am I wrong?"*

Despite it all, though, Chiho kept her eyes on him, keeping her head up and glaring strong as she fought against the cruel force.

But then...

"So shall it be."

With a dignified-sounding voice and a loud crash, Libicocco's body disappeared from in front of Chiho. The devilish force surrounding him faded away, easing Chiho's mouth and throat.

"Gn...nnh...!!"

He was now in midair, wings spread wide as he growled at where Chiho was.

"I am, more or less, another one of the new generals. And I happen to not like this, thank you very much, and so I *will* stop you by force," a certain cleric said.

A giant hammer swung breezily through the air, making the rain splashing around it sparkle in the rays of sunlight beaming down.

"S-Suzuno!" Chiho shouted with her freed lungs.

Suzuno, her hairpin transformed into her trademark weapon, let her rain-drenched hair blow in the wind as she turned her eyes to Chiho, safely ensconced behind her.

"My apologies for being late. The storm wall suddenly grew stronger, and penetrating it proved a trial."

"Dude, if you put it that way, it sounds like you got through it all by yourself!"

Another familiar voice from above them. Turning around, Chiho was just in time to see Urushihara land on the roof, white wings folded behind him. Their color stymied her.

"Urushihara... Is that...?"

They were no longer the jet-black that they were during the battle against Maou. They were a radiant, angel-like white. He turned his back to her, resentful at what she was paying attention to.

"Dahh," he groaned. "If I knew he was gonna try kicking this much ass, I woulda focused more on filling up my demonic force."

"Do not even joke about that, Lucifer," Suzuno warned, eyebrows furrowed in dismay.

"I'm not joking," came the cool reply. "But let's forget about that for today, okay?" Urushihara looked up at Libicocco, freshly bashed into the air by Suzuno. "That guy opened up a Gate and landed here in this school. That can't be a coincidence. I gotta admit, I feel kinda at fault for this."

"As do I?"

"Huh? ...What?"

Suzuno and Urushihara both took a breath—coming off as a highly unlikely team to Chiho—and then turned back to Libicocco. He was clutching the side of his body Suzuno's hammer hit as he gradually landed on the roof.

"...Lord Lucifer, and...the Scythe of Death?"

"Mm?" Suzuno lifted an eyebrow. "You know me?"

"Yes. You match the description that dung-beetle Farlo gave me. And..."

"And what?"

"No... It is simply unexpected, is all. If you are here..."

Suzuno's gut feeling told her that Libicocco's force was either on a par with hers or maybe a tad weaker. That surprise strike from the rear must have taken the wind out of his sails. And with Urushihara as her more-or-less ally, there was little chance of defeat even with a full-frontal approach. Maou was on his way, too, for that matter.

So why was Libicocco acting like he didn't have a care in the world?

"...Then this couldn't have worked out any better."

The malice behind his grin was like nothing before it.

❋

""""......""""

Now there were three people silently watching each other around the table. The new one had trouble kneeling for extended periods of time, so he sat with his legs crossed instead, dressed in a shirt and pants he borrowed from Ashiya.

"So, uh, who's this?"

"I have no idea."

Ashiya had given tremendously wishy-washy answers to Rika's questions so far, but on this one, he was decisive. This man that Maou ejected into the room during his whirlwind entrance and exit—one Ashiya couldn't even begin to conceive a believable explanation for—he had truly never seen in his life.

Between his looks, what little conversation they had made, and the way a flying Maou deposited him into the room uninvited, it seemed safe to assume he wasn't Japanese. The first possibility that came to mind was that he was from Ente Isla, but Ashiya wasn't entirely sure of it. The mystery man wasn't projecting holy or demonic force of any kind—so why would your normal, everyday, average joe of an Ente Islan be hanging out in Japan?

One thing Emi, Suzuno, and Emeralda all had in common—Sariel and Gabriel, too, on the other side—was that they all had superhuman abilities, not to mention the skills needed to traverse between worlds. They had a means, in other words. If this man was just a normal Ente Isla citizen, how did he get here? He didn't have that kind of ability, and yet, here he was.

Ashiya flashed Rika a glance.

"Ms. Suzuki?"

"Hmm?"

"I apologize, but I will have to leave you out of this for a few moments."

"Huh?"

Ashiya apologized to her again in his heart, turned to the man Maou just brought in, and opened his mouth.

<"Do you understand this?">

The man blinked, then eagerly nodded. <"Common Vezian…? No, Centurient, is it not? You aren't from this nation, either?">

"Umm??"

Rika's eyes opened wide at the sight of these two men speaking a language she had never heard before.

<"That man, Maou; he was just the same, no? Who are you people?">

<“To be honest, I’d like to ask that of you first. You do not appear to be a spellcaster. Why are you here, in this world, now? Who are you?”>

“Um, hang on a second, guys…”

<“It would take too long to explain. As you say, I know nothing of magic. I used to be a farmer. In an ideal world, I would have spent my entire life without setting foot outside the rural edges of Saint Aile.”>

“What language is that…?”

Rika’s eyes spun. It wasn’t English, and it wasn’t the German or French she occasionally heard snippets of in news broadcasts or documentaries. It sounded like something from outer space to her. She couldn’t figure out where one syllable ended and the next began.

<“There is not much else I can say. Not so long as I don’t know who you or Maou are. However, I crossed into this world because I am charged with protecting this child…Tsubasa. She is to be given to another person, someday.”>

<“Given…?”> This puzzled Ashiya. He recalled the girl Maou seemed to be traveling with. <“Is Tsubasa…the young woman Maou brought with him?”>

<“…”>

When it came to people in his life named after the word for “wing”—as *tsubasa* meant in Japanese—Ashiya could think of another person. Someone who crawled around this room for a whole week before coming under their mortal foe’s guardianship—and was now just as missing as she was.

<“Well. Now I know why Maou saw fit to bring you here. Although…I suppose you aren’t as important as this Tsubasa woman, eh?”>

Ashiya sharpened his words. He would allow no room for lies or denials.

<“This woman is a personification of a Yesod fragment, is she not?”>

<“…”> The man fell silent again. But he didn’t avert his eyes.

It had not been that long ago. Camio, the Devil Regent, told them what Olba had told him—that there was another holy sword, located right here in Japan, and Ciriatto was on the hunt for it.

Ashiya couldn’t hide the excitement coursing through his body.

In this simple ex-farmer, there existed the potential key to changing the very fabric of reality within Ente Isla.

<"You… You're…">

He tried to keep the agitation from his voice. His mind was full of haphazard guesses, and he needed to take action on them.

<"Are you…the father of Emilia Justina?">

"…Emilia?"

This familiar-sounding word, the first she could understand, unnerved Rika. Both of the men noticed the reaction. They couldn't blame her for it.

<"Then you're… Ah, is that it?">

<"So it is. What a state of affairs…">

Thus Nord Justina, father of the Hero, and the Great Demon General Alciel of the Devil King's Army made their hellos.

<"So you're… It couldn't be. Is that Maou person the…the 'chosen one' my wife talked about?">

<"'Chosen one'…?">

<"That was how she put it. 'When the chosen one is ready to reveal the truth behind the world,' she said, 'my daughter must be given her wings.' I had my suspicions when Maou mentioned Emilia's name.">

This presumably meant Laila, the archangel they knew to be Emi's mother. But although the angels were supernatural in nature, their existences were just as common and vulgar as anyone else's. They didn't have the power to alter destinies and bind the earth by magic with a few choice words, as they were portrayed in the old legends and scriptures. And why would a mere archangel go around calling the Devil King Satan the "chosen one"? Nothing sounded more arrogant to Ashiya.

"Um…"

And what about this "truth behind the world" nonsense? Lofty-sounding words, to be sure, but what "truth" can there be behind something as nebulous as the world? Anyone claiming such a thing is about as worthy of one's trust as a jewelry appraiser or an "expert panelist" on a cooking game show.

"Hey, guys?"

Where does a single human being—with a single angel at his side—get off, really, acting all high and mighty about some nonexistent "truth"? Demons like us have no time for such lofty malarkey. It is no more valuable to us than a pebble on the side of the road.

"*Listen* to me!!"

"Ahh?!"

Ashiya leaped up at the sound of someone screaming, holding a surprised hand against his ear. Rika, looking more demonic than most demons, was by his side.

"I don't know what the two of you are figuring out by yourselves, but you mind lettin' me in on some of it?"

"Uh..."

"You are quite...scary woman, aren't you?"

Even Nord could tell that Rika being given the outsider treatment was enraging her. His attempts at assuaging her were met with the same cold eyes that slew Ashiya a moment ago.

"Listen, man, if you want to live out your natural lifespan in Japan, try not to be so honest all the damn time, okay?"

"Oh..."

"So, Ashiya?"

"Y-yes...?"

"When're you gonna tell me who this guy is and why Maou and Urushihara and Suzuno can all *do* stuff like that?!"

Ashiya didn't complain about having that muddle of questions thrown at him all at once. It'd result in blood if he did, he knew. But even before Maou floated in, he had already made up his mind.

"M-Ms. Suzuki." Ashiya brought his arms out, attempting to place them on Rika's shoulders to soothe her. "I promise I will tell you, so will you please sit down for a—"

"That's not gonna help you get away from me."

"Hm?"

Rika had been about ready to throw fireballs at Ashiya. Now, it was her own cheeks that burned a hot red. Dejectedly, she followed his instructions, all but collapsing to the floor. "So?" she glared as she looked upward. "What is it?!"

Ashiya demurred for a moment, unsure where to begin. Then he pointed at Nord.

"So this man…"

"Y-yes?"

"Apparently he is Yusa's father."

"Okay……wait, what?"

She almost walked right through it before her mind backtracked. Her eyes were like tiny dots as she pointed them at Nord. "Emi's… father?"

"Indeed. I believe it is likely the truth."

"Wh…What? So, is…?" Emi's face went a little pale as she recalled the abuse she lobbed at Ashiya. "Well, I, I apologize for being so rude, then."

"Oh, is fine. I am rather, ah, in dark myself."

Ashiya wondered if it was such a good idea for Nord to be so forgiving, but decided dwelling on the topic would be fruitless.

<"This woman is one of Emilia's friends in this nation. Her name is Rika Suzuki.">

"Rika…?"

"Um, yes?"

"You've helped Emilia for me… Thank you."

He made it sound like Emi was receiving in-home care from Rika or something, but she didn't comment on it. She could tell what he meant between the words.

"Oh, no, thank *you* very much… Um, Ashiya?"

"Yes?"

Rika looked up at him after bowing politely at Nord for no real reason.

"You guys have both been saying 'Emilia' a lot, and that's what her dad just called her now, so, um…"

An honest answer to this would end it all. It would mean putting Rika in the same boat as Chiho. Chiho was accepting enough, but what about this girl? Slowly, Ashiya began to weave the words that were destined to change Rika's life, fully aware in his mind that he might have to call upon Suzuno to erase her memories later if things failed to work out.

"I mean… Is it kinda like how Japanese people give nicknames to themselves if they're living overseas so people pronounce their names right? Or, like, something based on religion, or a middle name or something?"

"No." Ashiya spoke slowly, trying to make sure Rika understood every word on a deep, personal level. "It is the real name of the woman you and I know as 'Emi Yusa.' Her full name is Emilia Justina."

"…Um, I'm not sure I follow." The bewilderment was obvious on her face. "Her real name? Emilia Ju…Justina? That's Emi's real name?"

"Yes."

"So Emi isn't Japanese?"

"That would be the case, yes."

"…Oh. *Ohh.* So if her dad isn't either, so is it kind of… Like, she was born and raised elsewhere, but then she immigrated to Japan and took a Japanese name like a pro soccer player or something?"

Ashiya had predicted this. Rika was trying to frame this situation in a way she could comprehend.

"No, not like that. Yusa's… Well, Emilia's homeland exists nowhere on this planet."

"…What do you mean?"

"Well, before that… Do you watch movies very much, Ms. Suzuki? Or play video games, for that matter?"

This seemingly unrelated question made Rika grow suspicious. "Wh-where'd *that* come from? I haven't played games much since I was kid, but I go to the theater pretty often, yeah."

"Then perhaps I could put it this way to help you understand the concept. Yusa Emi, or Emilia Justina, is not an…well, an Earthling, exactly."

"A what?"

"This is not quite the correct way to phrase it, but to put it simply, Yusa is an alien from outer space. She comes from another world, one far away from here… One that exists nowhere on Earth."

"…Are you screwing with me?"

It was a completely understandable response. He anticipated this, as well; this anger-tinged reaction. For the average human being, it was a completely natural response.

"If you are unable to believe me, Ms. Suzuki, then I am afraid I will be unable to explain the phenomena you just saw."

"Just saw...? Wait." Rika suddenly looked out the window again. The rain was thudding against it even harder now. The very one Suzuno and Urushihara flew out of. The one Maou appeared from, then soared right back through, into the sky.

"From here, to the house over there, it's got to be at least thirty feet. Do you think there is any human being who can manage that?"

"..."

Her eyes darted between Ashiya and the window several times. Seeing these incomprehensible events made her mind incapable of accepting the truth behind them. Perhaps things would be different if reality, in all its vivid intensity, was thrust before her all at once. But Rika didn't know anything before today. And she had seen only a snippet of the truth.

"Ms. Suzuki."

"Ahh...!" Rika froze, throat emitting a long groan. "Ah... Ah, ah..."

Ashiya could tell the firmness of the past was gone—in its place, a paralyzing fear of the unknown world she had gained access to. She probably couldn't speak if she'd tried.

"B-but how could that...? No way! I mean, Urushi... Suzuno... Maou..."

She turned over the events she saw, one by one, as the names came out. Yet, the stoutness of her heart drove her to continue defending the fortress of common sense that watched over her brain.

"I-I mean, that's crazy. Are you kidding me? This has to be a load of crap. How am I supposed to believe that? Like, I'd believe you more if you said Suzuno and all of 'em are magicians or some kinda ESP masters or something! At least you could claim *those* exist in the world..."

"Indeed. If I were in your shoes, Ms. Suzuki, I think I would say the same thing."

"Sh-show me some kinda evidence! Like, why're you saying you're all space aliens if you're working part-time and living hand to mouth like this?!"

"...I have no defense for that," snickered Ashiya, despite it all. "But even 'space aliens' have to sing for their supper, you see."

This was exactly why, if something like this hadn't happened, he never would've wanted to reveal himself to Rika. But these were all people from other worlds. People who had no business running into each other in the first place. Ashiya reverting to demon form would be all the evidence he needed, but that was far beyond his grasp right now.

"I regret that I cannot provide conclusive evidence to you at the moment...but how about this? Once Suzuno Kamazuki returns home, I promise I will have her prove it to you. Assuming, Ms. Suzuki, you are willing to listen to this so-called ridiculous tale to the end?"

"..."

Rika gave him a look of sheer doubt.

<"I cannot blame her for her disbelief,"> Nord whispered. <"I would have laughed it off if someone on Ente Isla told me about this other world, with its civilization advanced beyond all imagination.">

Ashiya internally agreed with him. A nation, a world, a civilization of human beings. Everything about Japan was a faraway dream of the future, one that demons, for all their supposed dominance and superiority over mankind, would never have for themselves.

<"Did Maou tell you about who *we* are?">

<"...No. But I imagine, at least, that he is not human.">

Come to think of it, Ashiya hadn't even given Nord his name yet.

Emi's disappearance, and Nord's subsequent arrival, seemed to symbolize in Ashiya's mind that the doomed, yet boundlessly comfortable day-to-day life they'd enjoyed in Devil's Castle was about to fall apart.

<"You are lucky, though...for I think I may need to have you introduce yourself the next time we meet.">

"Huh?"

Nord, silently following Ashiya and Rika's argument up to now, suddenly stood up, a gruff look on his face. The long-sleeved ROCK ON SASAHATA! T-shirt he was wearing (won by Ashiya in a drawing at the local shopping center) wasn't a match for his demeanor, but it didn't stop him from soundlessly padding over to the window. The building rattled anyway, as Ashiya's gaze followed to the window.

The sight made him instantly tense. There, inside the typhoon-level storm, there shouldn't have been a single person. But now, there were many.

<"We're fully surrounded. I haven't seen them before. Do you know what force they belong to?">

Ashiya could answer this question. He *could*, but the answer was still not one he could fully *believe*. Had his world ever engaged in behavior as reckless as this before?

<"The armaments come from...the Knights of the Inlain Azure Scarves, second in rank among the eight knight corps that serve Efzahan of the Eastern Island. What is the meaning of this?">

Ashiya had directed the question more at himself than Nord.

The entire apartment building had been completely surrounded by a dizzying number of knights in exotic-looking uniforms. When did they show up? And from where? More assassins sent by Barbariccia, like with Ciriatto? No. The knights stationed outside were all human. Ashiya could detect no particular magic from them. And although he didn't know what for, it was clear they were after everyone inside the building.

"Wh-what? What's up with you two now?"

Ashiya's mind instant sprang back into reality. Depending on how the political cards worked out, there was always going to be the chance that the human world would aim their sights on him, Maou, Urushihara, Nord—even Suzuno. But Rika was different. She was a Japanese woman, completely uninvolved with the affairs of Ente Isla. He couldn't draw her in to that world; he couldn't drag her into this battle.

<"This has nothing to do with Miss Rika,"> Nord said. <"We have to protect her. Don't we?">

<"Y-yeah,"> Ashiya said, nodding.

<"Are they after me...? I doubt it. I wouldn't be here if I had not met Maou earlier. So are they after you?">

<“It would have to be. It could be our neighbor, perhaps, but either way, we’re the only three people in the building now.”>

The ominous army outside showed no signs of movement, but with their numbers, a human-wave attack would be all it took to finish Ashiya off.

<“Can you fight?”>

<“Under any normal circumstances, I could finish off these forces in an instant. Now, however…”> Ashiya clenched his teeth. It all felt so pathetic to him.

<“I, too, have never received any formal battle training. If Tsubasa… If only Acieth were back here for us…”>

This Tsubasa, or Acieth, must have been the woman with Maou earlier. A woman who was probably zooming to Chiho’s aid at the moment, for reasons Ashiya couldn’t fathom.

Then he realized. If everyone in the forces surrounding them were from the Eastern Island, there was only one man who could’ve pulled the strings behind them: Olba Meiyer. And with Emi gone and Chiho’s school under attack by someone or something, either Suzuno was coming to the rescue, or Maou—whose powers were near infinite, assuming he could get his act together. Urushihara’s motives remained a big question mark, but Ashiya knew there were times when he tapped on a resource besides demonic force to wield his powers.

It meant that no matter how he put it, there was only one force in Japan right now with absolutely zero ability to fend for itself.

“The Eastern Island…?”

Ashiya gritted his teeth. Emi and Suzuno weren’t the only ones in danger. The furor over at Chiho’s school was just a feint. Olba and Barbariccia, their enemies, had their swords pointed squarely at the Great Demon General, Alciel.

*

“Uggh, this rain is awful… It wasn’t like this at all on the other side.”

The woman who left the Sasazuka Station building groaned at the driving rain as she surveyed her surroundings.

"Should I grab a taxi? I don't think it's that far from the station, though. It'd kinda be a waste."

She stood in front of a neighborhood map as she pondered over which road to take, a wheeled travel suitcase with a large shoulder bag slumped on top of it at her side. But the piece of paper she held in her hand wasn't some handwritten map, or note, or cell phone. It was, oddly enough, a résumé.

"Right! Taxi it is! I don't wanna get all wet!"

She stuffed the wrinkled-up résumé in her shoulder bag, walked through the hall that housed the turnstiles, arrived at a guardrail on the side of the road, and looked around for an open taxi.

Then the wind changed direction.

"Agh!"

She twitched her nose a little.

"...What is *that*?" she said, puzzled. She rubbed her chin for a moment in thought, then turned toward the direction from which she detected a certain scent.

"Ahh..."

She nodded, her suspicions apparently confirmed. It noticeably soured her face.

"Can't take the taxi there, huh? Shoot. They don't have a bath, either, do they?"

Then she trudged back into the station, still griping to herself as she tossed her possessions into a coin-op locker. After that:

"Hyaaaaaahhhhh!!"

She screamed as she plunged, running, into the heart of rainy Sasazuka, without so much as an umbrella to protect her. Her carelessly tied ponytail and healthy tan were both instantly soaked, and it wasn't long before she melted into the long curtain of water before her.

⁂

Maou and Acieth, meanwhile, were finally near Sasahata North High School, despite their little side trip. They were encountering a few difficulties.

"Arrrrgghh!!"

Maou screamed as he tried battering his way through the storm-wall. But his human legs couldn't even keep him upright against the pounding gale. It sent him reeling along the road before he crashed into a light post.

"Owwwww!"

"Wow, big disaster!" Acieth observed, not bothering to comment on Maou's painful misfortune.

"*Damn* it! We made it all the way here and I can't even see inside!"

From the outside, it looked like a gigantic cumulonimbus cloud had decided to swallow up the school grounds. It had settled in a neat circle around the property, refusing entry from the outside to anyone and anything. The damage outside this area was far below what he feared—just one (rather recently) downed light post, actually.

Things, however, were different inside the school grounds.

"You are no help at all, huh, Maou?"

"Man, do I hate you."

Acieth shrugged, not even bothering to care about her hair slapping all around her head. "Why you tell me to go back to apartment anyway? I no like that."

"Well, if something happened to you or Nord, we'd *really* be up the creek!"

Figuring that transport was the hard part and he could get together with Suzuno to handle the rest of the dirty work, Maou had ordered Acieth to return to Devil's Castle and await further instructions. But:

"Are you suuuuure? It is better if I here?"

"You are really pissing me off right now!"

Maou just couldn't get in the school. Once the local wind speed surpassed forty miles an hour or so, it was hard for a normal human being to even stand up. The wind around this storm was a lot faster than that—going in unprotected would just send him careening back all over again.

"Wonder if Suzuno's already in there," he muttered nervously. He didn't know what kind of enemy was lurking inside, but recent otherworldly visitors to Japan were proving to be quite a handful to the Devil King, especially in his current inconvenienced state. The sort of foe that not even the Hero could handle without Alas Ramus would (he hated to say) give Suzuno some mean odds to deal with.

Along those lines, Maou had yet to actually see Suzuno devote her all to a fight. He had seen that from Emi after their knock-down-drag-out on Ente Isla, and there was no doubt Alas Ramus had made her even stronger. But while Suzuno had been his enemy at one point, Maou was equipped with nothing but a pair of boxers at the time, and Suzuno was clearly restraining herself. Her full powers as a magical warrior remained a mystery to him. He wondered how often Church clerics engaged in all-out combat in the first place, not counting exceptions like Olba—but even back in Choshi, she was going on about how she wanted to kill an entire army of Malebranche down to the last man.

Maou tried to spot her amid the storm, but the howl of the wind and the pattering of the rain, along with the sirens from fire engines all around the neighborhood, made it impossible. The stormwall was already exacting nearly its full force by the time he arrived. It made sense that someone called the authorities to deal with this bizarre weather event. Not that it was Maou's fault, but it'd still be nice, he thought, if Japan's general public was willing to accept this as just another freak climate event to argue about online.

"Hmm... Over there."

"Huh?!"

As Maou descended further and further into panic mode, Acieth unexpectedly pointed at a speck in the air.

"There. Traces from opening."

"Where?!"

There was no telling where she was pointing to, what with the stormwall, the wind, and the assorted other detritus flying through the air.

"It is demon-force wind. I think someone forced it open, there. One more push, and I think they smash up the whole thing, huh?"

"Whaddaya mean, one more push? Who?"

"Wow, Maou, why you so useless? All right. I'll do it. You want go inside, yes?"

"You…can do that?"

"Mmm… Can you give me little more time? Pop isn't near me, so…"

"Pop" didn't seem to have a lot of holy energy storage potential within him. What was the deal with that?

"How much time are we talking?"

"Mmm…one hour?"

Maou almost fell for entirely non-wind-related reasons.

"That's too damn long! It'd be faster to just go back and fetch Nord again!"

"Wanna do that?"

"I told you, I don't wanna get you guys involved in this crap."

"Ooh, but it'll take big power to break that down…and if you were my latent force, Maou, I think that doesn't make holy power for me."

"Latent what?"

"Force. My sister and me, our power comes from person serving as our latent force. The strength in heart, yes?"

"Whoa, hang on!"

That sounded like something extremely important, this little tidbit she just tossed at him. He wanted to explore it more fully, but he could tell listening to the whole story would take even longer than an hour.

"Just give me a quick synopsis, okay? Are you saying you can siphon power from someone right by you? Even someone like Nord with no magic force at all?"

"Mmm, not sucking from him, no. More, um, his influence makes me feel better?"

Maou gasped. It was exactly how he transformed into his full demon self. By turning the feelings people felt in their minds into actual power.

"Well, can you make me the target for the time being or something?!"

"Ooh, yes," Acieth said, quickly nodding, before suddenly switching over to a dour frown. "But I dunno… I don't like your feeling, Maou. Not sure if I can *accept* you, or…"

"How you can say that? This is an emergency! And, geez, it's only the first time we've met!"

Never in his time in Japan had someone so brightly, cheerfully stated to him that he was physiologically unacceptable to her. She had *just said at the test site* how swell his hand smelled, too!

"But you can do it, right?"

"Mmm, but it is no holy force from you, Maou, so…"

"It doesn't matter! We just gotta apply as much power as we can to that rift you mentioned, right?"

"Yeaaah…"

Acieth still seemed reluctant. Maou grabbed her hand, clenching at it.

"Ah!"

"Please! We have to try something! I'll take care of *you* after that!"

"R-really…? That, first time a man said that to me…"

Acieth's cheeks had just a twinge of pink to them.

"…I mean," Maou nervously added, "I'll tell you everything I know about your 'sister,' all right?"

"All right. Go a little closer."

Acieth motioned with her eyes as Maou took a step forward, figuring there was some sort of process he had to follow.

"S-sure, I… Whoa!"

Instead, what he found was Acieth, eyes closed, bringing her face right up to his. He hurriedly sidled back.

"Wha-wha-what're you doing?!"

"What? It is forehead and forehead, yes?" she replied, clearly surprised by this sudden rejection.

Maou breathed a sigh of relief. It wasn't quite the worst he had feared. But then, he realized exactly the extent of what he had just imagined. It filled him with an inscrutable sort of shame.

He approached Acieth again, this time carefully, as he brought his head forward.

"No running, now."

"Yeah, yeah," Maou said, smirking a little at how Acieth phrased the command like a line from an action flick.

Her forehead approached his. As it did, he spotted a familiar glow. It was purple, and just like with Alas Ramus, it came from her Yesod fragment. So Acieth really *was* like Alas Ramus.

"Your latent force, huh…?"

Just as Acieth's phrasing crossed his mind again, their foreheads met. Then, the next moment, it was Acieth jumping back, like she just touched something hot.

"Wh-what is it…?" Maou grew nervous. Was it some kind of problem with the procedure, he wondered, as Acieth gave him a look of shock like nothing he'd seen before.

"M-Maou…" she said with trembling lips. "You… You're…"

"Yep."

Acieth's forehead gave out a stronger pulse of light.

"You *were* Devil King?! Like, 'Maou' in Japanese? So you have that last name?!"

"Oh, for…"

Whether an Idea Link–style force sprang into action or their little love tap triggered a little demonic force, Acieth must have learned the truth just now. Something about her reaction, however, made the moment seem less than dramatic. Yes, his name meant exactly what it sounded like.

"*That's* what surprises you at this point?! What's the big problem, huh? Use your ears, geez!"

"It not very creative, no!"

"Oh, *you're* one to talk… Yow!"

Before Maou could continue pleading his argument, the light from Acieth's head extended across his entire body.

"Ay, look at me, leaving body and soul to King of All Demons… I'm sorry, Mom…I am bad daughter to you…"

"Dude, I'm not some street punk asking your mom to let me date you, all right?!"

Acieth never failed to seize the opportunity to berate Maou. But now all the light made her practically invisible to him.

And then, it exploded.

"Agh!!"

Acieth was now an array of countless light particles, each still strengthening more in power—and they were all descending upon Maou.

"Uh… What's…? This isn't…?"

Beyond the initial surprise, Maou's brain was warning him about potential disaster ahead. As the light enveloped him, he realized he had seen something quite a bit like this before. Quite a few times, actually. Although it was the other way around whenever he saw it.

"…This is exactly like when Alas Ramus comes out of Emi, ain't it?"

It was probably too late, in assorted ways, by the time the thought reached his mind. That was because the pillar of purple of light at the base of the stormwall was tearing through the sky, all but ready to rip it apart.

❈

A dull clanging sound echoed across the Sasahata North High School area as Suzuno's hammer thudded against Libicocco's dire claws.

But the cross-dimensional battle unfolding in the sky didn't quite have Chiho's full attention. She glanced at Urushihara, standing on the roof as he watched the fight, and the door back downstairs, ripped open by Libicocco a while back. The twisted knob was still on the floor.

"Stop worrying, dude," Urushihara said, noticing Chiho's eyes on him. He gave the steel door a couple of pats to reassure her. "I can seal this door back shut with holy force, easy."

"Y-yeah, hopefully…"

It still worried Chiho to no end. Urushihara was, after all, a fallen angel—one whose lifestyle fit the term perfectly—and she assumed he was more of a demon in terms of species by now. The white wings, and the power on a level of Emi's or Suzuno's, was nothing short of astonishing to her.

Suzuno must've spotted him a 5-Holy Energy β—but was he safe drinking that? It was the same as what Chiho drank, although her dosages were still being strictly regulated. Just one of those little bottles was enough to send the (allegedly) mighty demon Ashiya into a near coma. Maou himself mentioned that an unexpected influx of holy energy would do nothing to his body but damage it.

Then she heard a voice from beyond the door, perhaps responding to Urushihara's rapping.

"Hey! Somebody out there?! Open the door! Dammit, why ain't it opening?!"

It was one teacher or other, boldly stepping up to take action despite the fierce typhoon and the Biblical conflict unfolding over the front yard.

Urushihara, following Suzuno's orders, had used his magic to seal off every door and window in the entire school. It was a preventative measure to keep any wayward students from getting caught up in the conflict, but the fact Urushihara engineered the spell gave Chiho no end of anxiety.

"Sealing an entryway's pretty high-level stuff, dude. A regular person could, like, never break through it."

The fact Urushihara had such an eerily convenient spell on hand was one surprise. She wasn't entirely sure what the spell was created for, either.

"Oh, there's a thousand 'n' one uses," he explained. "Maybe you don't know, living in Japan and everything, but folks like kings and Church officials cast this spell on themselves and their, like, treasure rooms and their sanctuaries to keep intruders away."

"I...see..."

It made sense to her. But why did Urushihara have it? And how did he cast it using holy force?

"Hey, it's not just me. Sariel and Gabriel can probably use it, too. It's kinda a must-have if you wanna call yourself a high-level angel. That's what he told me, at least, so I learned it."

"Told you?"

This puzzled Chiho for a moment, but Urushihara's attention was focused back on the fight. No further explanation seemed forthcoming, so she joined him instead.

It didn't take long for even her to conclude that the battle was decidedly one-sided. Despite the bulky-looking kimono, Suzuno wasn't letting the demon so much as touch her. All the bravado Libicocco attempted to dominate Chiho with was long gone—after all the abuse it had taken, the claws on one of his arms had been taken fully out of commission.

During that first battle she witnessed between Emi and Urushihara, there were so many spells and complex battle strikes exchanged that it looked, to her eyes, straight out of a fantasy blockbuster. By comparison, the fight between Suzuno and Libicocco seemed kind of like a schoolyard brawl, or a round of backyard wrestling. It wasn't pretty, but watching Suzuno swing a hammer easily as tall as she was, smashing it against a demon that weighed several times as much as her, was undeniably a sight to behold.

And yet, it was clear to even Chiho's eyes that she was going easy on him. She had taken his back and overpowered him in a hammer-on-claw duel multiple times, but not once did she attempt to strike a lethal blow on Libicocco. She couldn't make it out from here on the roof, but they were exchanging more than a few words in the process, too. Maybe she was pleading with him to return home.

"...Huh. Weird."

"What?"

Urushihara, watching the proceedings above him, cocked his head. "Like, Libicocco sure doesn't fight like a Malebranche."

"What do you mean?"

"Well, dude, he sucks. He must not be going full bore on 'er."

"Is that maybe because he's in Japan, so he doesn't have access to his full powers and stuff?"

"If that's what it is, he better remove that storm barricade quick, or else he's going back home in three or four chunks. Like, ditching the rain and stuff would let him devote that demonic force to the fight, but why ain't he doing that? And that's not the only thing, either."

Good point. It was definitely Libicocco summoning this vast storm over school grounds. Diverting that energy in Suzuno's direction would certainly make the battle a little fairer for him.

"Wh-what else is there...?"

"I noticed this with Ciriatto, too. Why's he still in demon form?"

"Um…"

"Like, this isn't the kinda situation I had, where I had pretty much an infinite resource of negative energy to tap on all around me. A Malebranche leader's, like, middle management by my standards, dudette. They ain't got near the Devil King's power to retain demonic energy. So how's he still able to stay a demon while he's wasting all this strength on the storm? Something's totally gotta be up with that."

"…What's the big deal with that? If he was going full force, Suzuno might be in a lot more trouble, besides…"

Urushihara's argument seemed to be supporting Libicocco more than anyone else. But as far as Chiho was concerned, the weaker the adversary, the better.

"Naaah, I think Bell could whip his ass then, too. It wouldn't wind up this one-sided, I don't think, but still. As it is now, Bell's gonna lay the hammer down on him sooner or later. I just have no idea why he's putting himself through this."

"Why…?"

He was right. Libicocco's bewitching words made her forget about it, but he had opened up the Gate to Japan himself. It was hard to imagine he was relying strictly on a source of negative emotions he could never have counted on.

Camio had arrived looking for Maou; Ciriatto had come for the holy sword; Farfarello had tried to bring Maou and Ashiya back home. None of the demons who had traveled to Earth had ever fulfilled their missions, essentially. What was Libicocco even trying to do?

"I don't like how this is all unfolding when Emilia ain't here, either. Did that guy say anything weird to you before we showed up?"

"Weird…?"

The weirdest thing, without a doubt, was the little pronunciation lesson he'd given her. But there *was* something else. Chiho recalled the conversation of ten or so minutes ago. What did Libicocco say he was here to do?

"Actually...he said this was the kind of 'job' every demon dreams of... He wasn't here to kill people in the school. He just wanted to start a ruckus, and make it as conspicuous as possible... I think that's what he said. But he triggered a ton of lightning, too..."

"Oh, like those flashes just before we got in?"

"Huh? Yeah."

"It wasn't *that* neat, dude..."

"Oh?"

"I mean, there were two or three lightning bolts, but they all hit antennas and lightning rods 'n' stuff. Looked more like a short circuit than anything."

"Huh? It was a lot more than just that! There was this massive bolt across the sky, and I couldn't even keep my eyes open..."

And yet the nearby homes were far less damaged than either Chiho or Libicocco imagined. Chiho chalked that up to Japan's superior disaster preparedness, but...

"I think that was all just illusory magic. The Malebranche's really good at that stuff."

"I-illusory?"

"Yeah. Like, they conquered the Southern Island so quick because they used dirty tricks, dudette. They used necromancy and illusions to conjure up whole armies of zombies and ghosts and stuff. Then when all the humans were freaking out, it was pretty much open season. I'm guessing he set it up so you were the only one to see that flash or whatever. He'd need a crapload of demonic force to pull off the real thing."

"..."

"Now, the stormwall, though... That's real. A Malebranche conjuring up stuff like that's pretty impressive, I gotta admit. Must be one of the old-time bosses, if I had to guess. In that gang, Malacoda's way ahead of the bunch there, but apart from him, it's pretty much just street-hood dudes like Ciriatto. He ain't using near the amount of spells I did, right? Maybe he's just conserving his forces or something, but if so, I really don't get why he won't shut off the storm."

"Oh, you know..." Chiho racked her brains for an answer, impressed at Urushihara's wholly unexpected insight.

"He wanted it *conspicuous*, eh...? What was he trying to make us take our eyes off of, though?"

"Urushihara?"

"...Oh."

Chiho looked up at Urushihara's voice. Suzuno was up there, behind the back of a nearly limp Libicocco and gearing up to hammer him down onto the school roof.

"Hnnngh!!"

She put her all into that swing. It was a home-run blast, sending the demon hurtling like a comet down toward Urushihara. "Ooh, that ain't good," he said as he raised his arms.

"Nh! ...Rgh!" Libicocco groaned as he stopped in midair. If he hadn't stopped, he might've caved in the old school building's roof with his weight. Urushihara must have cast something to prevent that.

"Yo. Malebranche general. You know she ain't goin' all out on you, right, dude? I dunno what you're hiding, but you keep that up, and you're dead."

"Gnn...nnh..."

Whether he didn't want to talk or was too physically drained to, Libicocco could do nothing but squirm above Urushihara's hands.

"Whew," said Suzuno as she gently alighted on the roof. "All bark and no bite." She slowly walked up to Libicocco, flicking the blood off her hammer. "Now! Release the school from your accursed storm at once! If not, I will be forced to take your life, and I would like to avoid that if I could."

"*...Kill me if you want,*" Libicocco said in a tight, pained voice. "*You're human.*"

Suzuno shook her head. "I will no longer kill simply because my adversary is a heretic...or a demon."

"Suzuno...?"

"You could have fought on more of an even keel if you annulled your stormwall magic. You refused to listen to my repeated warnings. You have another objective you are hiding from me, yes?"

"..." Suzuno must have found Libicocco's behavior just as perplexing as Urushihara had.

"I will kill you only if I decide you have clearly and intentionally blighted the world and its people with your malice. I have learned how to be more flexible with my credo in Japan. I only fight an enemy that shows malice against me. The idea of killing yet again simply because our races or species differ sickens me."

"Heh...heh-heh... That 'credo' will come back to haunt you in the end."

"'Tis better to rue my betrayer than to rue the fact that I failed to believe in him. The human world has grown rather...complex as of late. I would hate to kill, only to wonder if my enemy was right the whole time."

Suzuno's hair, still wet from the rain, shone in the light around her.

"Besides," she said, "my friends are not such weak people that a single betrayal would mark the end for them."

With that, she shrank her hammer, returning it to hairpin form as she inserted it into a pocket. It would be too much trouble to put it on before her hair dried.

"...Am I wrong, Chiho?" she asked, turning around.

Chiho was dumbfounded. She knew exactly which of her "friends" she was talking about. She had always hoped Suzuno would come out with it, but she never imagined it actually happening.

"Y-yes... Yes, you're right, Suzuno!"

It made her supremely happy for some reason, swinging her fists in the air as she reflexively jumped up and down.

"Uh, y'know..."

Urushihara—who, it turned out, could read the atmosphere in a room a lot better than she thought—knew what they were getting at. He wasn't the sort of person to accept it that easily, but he was too lazy to rain on their parade, either.

"So what're we gonna do about these stormwalls—?"

Just as he attempted to move things along, Urushihara's sight was completely taken over by an intense light.

"Ah?!"

"What in the...?"

"Huh?"

The three of them looked up at the sky in order. The roof they were standing on had suddenly been engulfed in sunlight. The rain and wind streaming from the inside of the wall stopped, as if releasing the school from its barrage, and now the sun and blue sky were visible once more.

"...Uh, did you do something?" an accusatory Urushihara asked Libicocco. This couldn't have been natural. The stormwall itself was still up there.

"..."

But Libicocco refused to answer. Suzuno, eyes still upon him, shook her head. "I do not like this one bit. What will happen next?"

Urushihara squinted at the sun above him, its rays pummeling his face. He raised a hand up to block them. It looked like some sort of all-seeing eye, looking down upon them through the break in the storm.

"Hmm?"

There, in the sun, he spotted a tiny black speck, like a small piece of trash stuck to the surface.

"Whoa, there's something in the sun..."

The speck gradually, ever so gradually, grew in size.

Urushihara's eyes opened wide—one of the handful of times each year he ever bothered to look serious. Tossing Libicocco aside, he leaped over to Suzuno and Chiho.

"What...?"

"Urushi...?"

His sudden spring to action surprised them both, but before they could voice their concern:

"Hooff!!"

Urushihara's wings spread out wide, shining in the light. All the two women could do was gasp. A searing flame, like a science-fiction

light beam, had just crashed down on the spot Suzuno and Chiho were standing on.

"Lucifer!!"

And Urushihara had stopped it. His arms were out, and just as he did with Libicocco before, he had made the beam stop dead in the air a few inches over his hands, protecting the girls.

This, however, was a daunting task. His white wings could spread out no further, his entire body shining as he strove to defend himself, but waves of intense heat were making Suzuno's and Chiho's hair blow back behind them.

"*Ghh*... Ahh! Shit...!" Beads of sweat ran down Urushihara's forehead. "What the hell is he *thinking*?! Bell! Get Chiho Sasaki outta here! I can't hold this!"

"Grab on, Chiho!"

Without waiting for a reply, Suzuno all but tackled Chiho at the waist. Once she was safe in her hands, Suzuno leaped up and shot away from the roof at speeds that could very well make Chiho lose consciousness.

"Ooh...eh...!"

Scooped up into the skies at a rate that upturned her stomach, Chiho watched the scene below her. The roof door leading downstairs was starting to bend—a steel door, one that Urushihara's holy magic was supposed to have sealed off. *That* was how hot it must have been. Was he all right, dealing with that by himself? The temperature of this gigantic flamethrower was such that the diminutive Urushihara began to shimmer in the haze underneath the beam.

"Wh-what's that?!"

Suzuno had finally traveled high enough that they were free of the beam's range. She slowed down, but even from here, they couldn't see where the flame was coming from.

"Suzuno! How's Urushihara?!"

"I don't know! But if we go back down there, the heat would roast you, Chiho!"

"No way..." the schoolgirl moaned.

Then things got worse. Slowly, ploddingly, a gigantic shadow arose away from the beam. Libicocco, tossed aside a moment earlier, had revived himself.

"Suzuno! Look!"

"I know! I'm dropping you off in the courtyard, Chiho!"

Suzuno turned away from Urushihara and the flame, trying to take Chiho to as safe a place as possible. But:

"D-damn you all!!"

Somebody was there, in midair, to stop her. Someone that, to someone who had just been fighting a demonic visitor from out of nowhere, was unbelievable to her.

"N-no…!"

Chiho, in her arms, began to feel desperation set in.

"Out of our way now, Heavenly Regiment!"

The enemy refused to budge. There were five of them there, surrounding Suzuno to keep her from descending.

"N-not Gabriel again?!"

The Regiment were the soldier-servants of the angels themselves. They had visited Japan on a couple of occasions, serving as Gabriel's bodyguards.

"They bear different weaponry," Suzuno moaned. "Gabriel's fighters simply fought with whatever they could find."

All five of them were clad in heavy, thick-looking red armor that covered their entire bodies. In his hands, each bore an identical black metal trident. Clearly, this was a different level of cohesion from the ragtag bunch Gabriel tolerated.

Every barb on every trident was aimed at the two of them. The threat might not have meant instant death, but it was enough to make Suzuno's mind race. There was no way a Malebranche leader and a Heavenly Regiment platoon would just happen to show up at the same time. It meant only one thing.

"You… You've really done it…"

There was a tangible frustration in Suzuno's voice. She still had no idea what they wanted, but there was no turning away from reality now. The demons maneuvering in secret on the Eastern Island were receiving support from the heavens—the angels themselves. It was impossible to believe, and impossible to know why it was happening, but it was the only possible explanation left.

"Suzuno..."

"Chiho, don't move. Ahh, curse this body! I swore to myself I would let nothing faze me...!"

Chiho couldn't see it from Suzuno's arms, but the woman's voice was now starting to be laced with tears.

"The black tridents, and the red armor. Iron, and red. And Lucifer, damn him, he refuses to move an inch!"

Urushihara was now almost fully swallowed by the fire hurtling toward the roof. Suzuno took the chance to curse his name anyway.

"Archangel Camael! What are you trying to accomplish?!"

The two of them could now feel seething rage emanating from the Regiment. The reaction made it clear Suzuno was on target. And although this angel couldn't have heard Suzuno's voice:

"S-Suzuno!"

The flame attacking Urushihara silenced Chiho's scream as it swelled further in size.

"Gaaahhh!!"

As they and the Regiment watched, the little figure on the roof was blown away by the light and flash, falling to a rest just before the edge of the roof.

"Urushihara! Urushihara!!"

She doubted he could hear her, but Chiho just had to call out anyway.

And that still wasn't all of it. Libicocco, dragging his battered and bruised body, began approaching Urushihara. Chiho held her breath in horror.

Suzuno had just taken a step further toward Chiho's ideal world, but now... These insane new events had wounded her all over again. Did that mean everyone was going away?

"*Ngh...!!*"

Chiho looked upward, teary-eyed. Now she could clearly see the figure that had fried Urushihara up so thoroughly. Like his Regiment, he was in a red suit of armor. His body, while still not quite Libicocco's size, was every bit the hulking mass that Gabriel boasted.

"Hoh, man… I never dreamed you'd put up with this farce, dude…"

The unwanted baggage of Devil's Castle, his holy force used up and his body literally browned and ready for serving, was back to human form. Yet even in his sorry state, he never took his eyes off the sky.

"Shiiiiit, Bell and Chiho Sasaki's gonna kill me for this. I totally said you wouldn't take action, too."

"…"

Between the full-body armor and the full-face helmet, the silent figure looked more like a berserker captain than an angel.

"So… Camael. Why the change of heart?"

The archangel Camael ignored Urushihara's question. He looked at Libicocco, motioning with his head.

"…*Tch.*" Libicocco sneered. But he carried out the order anyway. It didn't involve Urushihara at all. Instead, he spread his tattered wings and began flying straight for Suzuno and Chiho.

"Sorry, you little ant."

Suzuno couldn't move, hampered in all directions by the Regiment. And unlike their private one-on-one meeting earlier, the look Libicocco gave Chiho was more awkward than anything else.

"Give it. You know the score."

Chiho looked down upon Libicocco's outstretched palm, scarred and missing a claw.

"The Yesod fragment. I know you've got it. Give it, and all of us are out of here. Now."

She found herself bringing a hand up to a pocket on her uniform.

"Don't do it, Chiho!!"

The subsequent scream from Suzuno made her freeze.

"Don't give them any more of the Sephirah! Remember what Gabriel and Raguel did to us!"

"B-but, Suzuno, Urushihara's been—"

"...If worse comes to worst, Chiho, I'll take your fragment and swallow it if I have to."

"And you think we demons would hesitate to dissect a human if need be?"

Chiho now found herself in the middle of a pitched war of words.

"It would beat simply handing it to you, any day of the week!"

Suzuno's voice was clearer now, more resolute. But the bravado was pointless now. All the two of them could hear in response was a cold, blunt command.

"...You heard her."

It was not aimed at the shouting Suzuno.

"Ngh!!"

"S-Suzuno?!"

Chiho could feel a dull impact run across her body. It was accompanied by a throaty groan from Suzuno.

"Ah...?!"

Then she saw something horrifying out from the corner of her eye. One of the Regiment's spears was sticking out of Suzuno's stomach.

"Suzuno!!" Chiho shouted. Before she stopped, she felt a strong momentum as Libicocco, who was right in front of her, shrank away. Suzuno had jumped back in midair.

"S-Suzuno?!"

"Do not worry about me," she replied, pained but resolute. "It was the butt end. *Hakk...!*"

"The butt end?!"

To Chiho, not all that familiar with midair warfare, all she could imagine was people's rear ends in her mind.

"Agh!"

She didn't have much time to dwell on the thought. A red Regiment member was advancing upon Suzuno, this time with the pointy end of his tri-tipped spear aimed at her.

"Curse youuuuuuuu!" Suzuno shouted in a fashion not befitting a cleric. She swept the tips away with her hammer, glided through the air to dodge them, and tried desperately to create more distance between her and the fighters. But it was for naught. They were far better trained than Gabriel's posse. Like the lead jet in a dogfight, one of them always made sure he was behind Suzuno's back; another kept his sights on Chiho, knowing full well she was the weak point. Yet another applied pressure from below, lest Suzuno attempt a landing.

And even if she managed to shake all five of them off, Urushihara was no longer able to stand—and Libicocco and Camael were still waiting.

"S-Suzuno! I—you...you don't have to worry about me, so..." Chiho, swung around in the air and barely able to take the g-forces, had to work hard to keep from biting her tongue as she spoke. "Go ahead and...and drop me, okay...? I don't mind if I'm hurt a little bit... It'll be, be easier to fight—"

"Silence!" Suzuno exclaimed as she threaded the needle in the air, executing an acrobatic maneuver to avoid another spear. "They are after you, Chiho, not I! If I let you go now, it will be the end for us both! ...*Ngh!!*"

The spear from another Regiment soldier grazed her leg.

"Suzuno!"

"D-damn it! Chiho, close your eyes!"

Without waiting for a reply, Suzuno softly chanted a spell, then swung her hammer at the soldier in front of her.

"Lightwave Flash!!"

The face of her hammer began to shine as brightly as the sun, blinding the soldier she targeted.

"Go awaaaaaaaay!!"

While his guard was down, Suzuno took a big swing and struck the soldier squarely in the pit of his stomach. She could feel the thud of the impact as the soldier disappeared from sight.

"Hang on, Chiho! We're moving!"

Before anything else, she had to escape the school. As it was, it was only a matter of time before students and teachers would be in danger. Urushihara's seal seemed to still be in effect, but Camael was just about to vaporize the entire roof of the old school building. She could protect Chiho alone, perhaps, but not the several hundred people currently on school grounds.

While Urushihara was still on Suzuno's mind, priority one right now was to keep Chiho and her Yesod fragment free from enemy hands. She zoomed in the air, almost causing Chiho to black out, before a sudden flash of light made her gasp in desperation.

"Sorry, pal, but your illusions won't work on Malebranche."

"Ngh?!"

The enormous body that stepped out from the light was Libicocco's. His remaining good claw was suddenly right in Suzuno's path. She couldn't avoid it. Instead she swung her hammer, slowing herself down as she attempted to smash the claw in her way.

"Graaaah!!"

Chiho, eyes seared by the light even through her eyelids and still about ready to pass out, heard Suzuno's scream just as she felt a warm liquid on her cheek. It made her consciousness literally white out. It should have been just a few seconds, but the next thing Chiho saw after the light fizzled and she came back to her senses was—

"…!!!!!!"

Chiho writhed as she let out a soundless scream. But her body didn't move. She couldn't move it, because now she was in Libicocco's arms. And Suzuno, who had tried too hard to bring her to safety…

"*…You just had to make this difficult, you little wench…*"

…was Suzuno, lying in the middle of the roof before Libicocco's eyes, covered in blood.

"S-Suzuno! Suzuno!!"

Even from her vantage point, Chiho could tell that something had cut deeply into her near the top of her shoulder. There was another slashing wound running from the visible part of her leg beneath the kimono. Fresh blood was gushing out of it.

But the worst part of it all was how her hair and kimono were both strewn across the concrete, kept in place by the Regiment soldiers that kept her down with their spears like they were performing a crucifixion. Her great hammer was now a powerless hairpin a few inches away from her hand.

"Ah…gghh… Chiho, *ngh…"*

But she was still trying to reach out to Chiho.

"Suzuno! …Agh!"

Chiho tried to reach out herself, but Libicocco was having none of it. He kicked Suzuno's outstretched arm away, looking down at her with a face that had almost a trace of pity on it.

"Why must you defy us so much? You're a Church cleric, no? He, and everyone around you, are all angels! The messengers of the gods, worthy of your unquestioning worship! What would you accomplish by defying them?"

Withstanding the pain, Suzuno glared at Libicocco, face drenched in blood.

"Angels… Angels willing to do things like this… I refuse to accept it! The only thing I worship is the path of righteousness… The path that leads us all to peace, and justice!"

The more she screamed, the more blood pumped out of her wounds. Chiho shivered, unable to speak.

"How can I accept angels who…who are willing to bargain with evil? Who hurt the people that serve them? Who bring chaos to the entire world?!"

"Very well. Warriors with a single-mindedness like that… I don't mind it. But there's nothing to do for it now."

The soldiers stepped up to Libicocco, as if summoned to him.

"Come on, you little ant. I'm not gonna ask you again. Give it."

The warning failed to reach Chiho's ears. All of her senses were paralyzed.

"Listen… *Koff koff!* Ch-Chiho… Never give it up…"

"S-Suzu…"

"I said, I'm not gonna ask you again. Do it, or you'll be damn sorry."

They were at the proverbial cliff, Libicocco and the soldiers advancing upon them—the hands of evil, posing as divinity.

*

"This... What the hell...is this?!!"

Rika's shout echoed across the streets of Sasazuka.

The rain grew stronger and stronger, soaking Villa Rosa Sasazuka's front yard. Accompanying the storm was the arrival of a group the likes of which she had never seen before—and for some reason, the phone she currently had in a death grip couldn't pick up any service.

"Ashiya! Nord!!"

And now Rika, sunken down on the wet ground, was watching the limp, wounded bodies of Ashiya and Nord.

"What's with you?! What's *with* you guys?!"

Rika, in a state of panicked confusion, threw her useless phone into the air. It bounced off the chest of the large man in front of her, the one who defeated Ashiya and Nord, and landed helplessly in a water puddle.

"Well, this sure got messed up. And here I thought having *the* Nord Justina was a total stroke of luck for me, too."

The man—standing out like the statue of some Greek god among the strange group—shrugged, a look of sheer disappointment on his face.

"I wasn't expecting any third parties here," he glumly muttered as he took a step toward Rika. "*Now* what'm I gonna do?"

"Ah, ah..."

Rika couldn't move, her legs failing her. She couldn't be blamed for it. A platoon of fully armored soldiers was scary enough of a sight—but this guy had just smashed Ashiya and Nord to the ground with a single swipe, right before her eyes. She could take a lot of things, but pure, unfiltered violence wasn't one of them. Her fear had frozen her solid.

"Man, I really don't like freaking girls out like this... Hey, uh, let me get one thing straight with you, mm-kay? I promise I don't want to hurt you or—"

"S-stay away! Stay away from me!! Help me! Ashiya, help me!!"

"...Geez, who do you think I am, anyway? I'm not a home invader or any—*ow!*"

The man winced at the piece of rock or whatever Rika had just picked up off the ground and thrown at him.

"...Well, yeah, guess it's too late for excuses, huh? ...Look, I'm sorry, mm-kay? You can cry or scream as much as you want, so just sit tight for a second, all right? ...Hey."

He signaled something to the group behind him. Four of the knights advanced toward him.

"Wait... Wait, what're you...?"

Rika watched as they picked up Ashiya and Nord, lying motionless on the ground.

"Where... Where're you taking them...?"

"Taking them? We're not taking them. We're returning them—back to where they came from."

"Where they...?"

"Ah, no need to worry about it. Oh, and don't bother going to the po-pos or anything, mm-kay? 'Cause we're kinda out of their jurisdiction, if you know what I mean. Just chalk it up as, 'hey, accidents happen,' y'know?"

"Ah!!"

"...Wait, huh?"

Although still too dumbfounded to speak, Rika suddenly found herself rising to her feet, walking up to the knight holding Ashiya, and grabbing him.

"Gah!"

"......!!"

"Wh-where're you taking him?! Quit giving me all this nonsense! Gimme Ashiya back! Give him *back*, goddammit!"

"Whoa, lady, come on! Can you knock that off? Geez, you spooked me..."

"Ah!!"

The knight finally managed to shake Rika off. She flew through the air before landing face-first in a puddle.

"Hey, whoa, uh...!"

Now it was the large man who sounded like he was in a panic. Not only did the knight release his grasp on Ashiya's body—now he had his sword out.

"Hold your frickin' weapon, you idiot! Don't make this more complicated for me!"

But the man was nowhere near close enough to the knight to stop him. Rika, on hands and knees, looked up to find a sight she never imagined seeing in her life in Japan—a weapon, an enraged knight, and her life ending right at this moment.

"Nh!"

She didn't even have the time to gasp. The weapon seemed to crawl in the air, glinting silver against the rain that tapped against it. But then:

"Hraaahahhh!!"

A scream penetrated its way through the air as the knight careened to the side like a rubber ball, just before the sword went all the way down.

"Whaa—?!" exclaimed the man, astounded beyond belief as the knight was plastered against the concrete-block wall that encompassed Villa Rosa Sasazuka. Slowly, ever so slowly, he crumpled to the ground.

"Wha…?"

The first thing Rika saw was a pair of feet clad in flat, rubber-soled shoes. Following the legs upward, she saw a pair of denim pants, posed in the tail end of a classic kung-fu kick. Farther up this person's body was a black shirt, tanned skin, and a black ponytail.

"…Who're you, huh?" Her assailant, so easygoing a moment ago, was now in a flustered panic. "And how'd you get in here?"

"How…?"

The woman, lowering her kicking leg with the grace of a kung fu movie star, was wholly unfamiliar to Rika.

"Since when did I need permission to horn in on *your* territory?"

She flashed an evil grin.

To a man, the rest of the knights, several dozen of them, unsheathed their swords and pointed them at the newcomer. The large man didn't stop them this time—but despite this threat, the tanned woman held her ground.

"Mess with me, and you'll pay for it with your lives, you got that? And that applies to you, too, mystery man."

"...Sure like talkin' big, huh? Who're you, anyway?"

"Well, I don't know this girl or that guy over there, so to put it simply..."

The woman turned her eye to Ashiya, still under close watch from the knights, and snickered to herself.

"I'm this Ashiya here's ex-boss."

⁂

As Suzuno's bloodstained consciousness faded, she watched in desperation as Chiho fell into the hands of the Regiment. She wanted to stop them, but she could no longer lift so much as a finger. All she could do was writhe in the pain her shoulder and leg were causing her.

Just as a Regiment soldier was about to lay hands upon Chiho, a beam of purple light, more powerful than the sun itself, burst from beyond the stormwall.

"*Wh-what?*"

"......?"

Both Libicocco and Suzuno—Camael, too, no doubt—turned toward the source of the light. It came from outside Sasahata North High's front gate.

"*Mngh!*" the demon moaned, fearing the new threat. His wall suddenly weakened by a considerable measure; the border that shut the school away from the rest of reality grew increasingly vague as the rain and wind simmered down. Soon, the entire wall was dismantled. The wind caused by this sudden change in barometric pressure was strong enough to knock down the entire Heavenly Regiment.

At that moment, the purple flash zoomed across the school grounds like a shooting star. The moment they all spotted it, the storm that had formed the wall up till now followed after it with intense momentum.

"*Huh...?*" Libicocco exclaimed as the light and the storm passed by his side. Then he realized his arm had started to feel oddly lighter. Or not lighter, exactly—

"*Agaaaahhhhhh?!*"

Libicocco's arm, the one he had used to grab the small girl before him a moment ago, was completely gone from the shoulder down. Blood spattered from his wound, coinciding with the intense pain that reached his head. He tried frantically to stop it as he fell to his knees.

"*Ah?!*"

Then he realized that the other human who was lying before him was now completely gone. The spears of the five armored soldiers charged with pinning her to the ground had been neatly sliced halfway down, like someone taking a butcher knife to a cucumber, and were now totally useless. The knights stared, dumbfounded, unable to parse what had just happened, before turning around to trace the path of the light and storm. It was a monster, and now it was standing in front of the downed Urushihara, protecting him. It was human in form, but its limbs, and the two horns on its head—one still partially severed—were unmistakably demonic.

"Ah...ah..."

Even though she was still being held by a demonic arm, the sense of serenity and safety Chiho felt now was more than enough to make the tears flow. It was Chiho's hero, the man who always stepped up for her in times of danger.

Sadao Maou now held Chiho and Suzuno in his arms. But not as the Devil King he once was. His height was the same as always. And unlike before, it did not physically pain Chiho to be near this demon—and demon he was, as shown by the legs and arms poking out from his UniClo outfit.

"M-Maou..."

"Sorry I'm late. I was kinda far away."

Maou didn't take his eyes off Libicocco and the Regiment, but the voice directed toward Chiho remained firm and strong.

Chiho nodded, the tears running down her already-wet cheeks.

"...It's...it's okay...*snif...*"

"You ain't hurt, are you?"

"No… Urushihara and…and Suzuno protected me…"

"Yeah?"

Maou gave her a gentle nod, then turned his attention toward Suzuno. "You are far…*far* too late, Devil King," she said before he could speak up, glaring with what consciousness she had left through the pain.

With Chiho in his left arm and Suzuno in his right, Maou gently dropped them off on the roof.

"I couldn't have possibly gotten here any faster, man," Maou sneered at Suzuno's unrelenting criticism. "At least I made it in time, okay? You could give a little thanks for that. Always darkest before the dawn and stuff."

Suzuno couldn't help but smile a little at that. Between Urushihara going down, Suzuno joining him, and the worst just about to happen to Chiho, it was the very definition of "dark."

"I would…appreciate it…if you left such dramatics to the Hero. Not you, Devil King…heh-heh…*ngh*."

Her face contorted as a wave of pain seized her. Her entire body was wounded and doused in blood—but she, and Urushihara, were both somehow still alive.

"You ain't dead, are you?" Maou asked, back turned. Suzuno shook her head lightly at the question, relieved—relieved that *Maou* was here, of all things—as the pain dominated her mind.

"It hurts enough to die…and the fact that it does means I am still safe."

Maou nodded. "Great job holding out for that long. I'll take care of the rest."

He was facing an archangel in the sky, a Malebranche leader in front of him, and five well-trained members of the Heavenly Regiment. He had the wounded Suzuno and Urushihara covered, as well as the helpless Chiho—but he still exuded an air of supreme confidence. He looked unarmed at first glance, his transformation to Devil King incomplete, and none of them felt any demonic force from him—and yet, Suzuno felt no anxiety at all. She felt safe, watching him from behind, and that confidence in him filled her heart.

"Right… I dunno what's going on here, really, but you guys were sure kicking some ass, weren't you? That's the first time I lost three Great Demon Generals in one go since Emi."

"Y-you…"

Maou sauntered up to the kneeling, armless Libicocco.

"You, you took my arm!" he screamed, still in shock that he had left his guard down around this half demon—the one who, even now, was grinning as he presented the severed arm to him like a prize.

"Well, look at this Malebranche wannabe, huh? Tryin' to act all tough around me, aren'tcha?"

The hand he had held out was surrounded by a purplish gleam.

"Mmm," Camael murmured to himself within his iron helm. It was the first time he had spoken so far, although no one else noticed.

The purple light ran from Maou's palm across his arm, eventually covering his entire body. Suzuno's eyes opened wide.

"It's not…demonic force…?"

It wasn't. There wasn't a trace of demon energy within Maou, even as he regained part of his original form and began to wield superhuman force once more. There wasn't any holy energy either, of course. It was just *power*, in its purest form, making Suzuno's own holy energy stir as it seemed to overwhelm her.

She had felt something like this before.

"Maou…?" Chiho said, voice weak but firm. She must have noticed something was different about Maou this time as well. Suzuno turned her eyes to her.

Then she remembered. She *had* seen this once, with Chiho. Over in the city of Choshi, far to the east of Sasazuka—at the Inuboh-saki Lighthouse, the first location in Japan to receive the rising sun's blessings each day.

"Well, then. Any of you guys willing to risk your life in battle as much as Emi is?"

Now there was something swinging in his right hand. Something filled to the brim with overwhelming strength.

"The...the Better Half... The holy sword!"

Everyone there—Libicocco, the Regiment, Camael, even Suzuno—called out the name. The sword in Maou's hand was every bit the carbon copy of the Better Half that was now inseparable from Emi's body.

*

"As far as I'm concerned, that guy over there's enough punishment for what you did to this girl. That's all I feel like doing, as long as you guys leave right now."

The tanned woman took a step forward, paying the large man and his army no mind as they seethed at him.

"Thing is, though..."

"...What?"

Somehow, there was something coming out from underneath her feet. It was billowing out, in fact, further separating them from the rain-shrouded neighborhood of Sasazuka.

"Mist...?"

"If you keep doing whatever you want to innocent bystanders like this, I'm not really in a position to let that slide."

"Ah!"

It was pressure, pure and simple. The woman's eyes shot right through the man's heart—and with it, a force that was neither demonic nor holy.

"I don't really care how your world winds up turning out. That's y'all's problem to deal with. But we took care of our business a long time ago. So if you start messin' around with all of our hard work..."

The woman let out a hard snort as she took a step forward, sending water flying.

"We aren't gonna take that sitting down, is what I'm sayin'."

That was all it took to make the knights stagger, struggling to handle the onrush of power.

"...?" It puzzled the mud-daubed Rika, who couldn't figure out why the knights edged away from her after seemingly no prodding.

She knew this woman was there to help her, but she doubted a lone woman could handle so many of these people at once.

Then things went in a completely unexpected direction.

"Okay. We'll go. Something tells me trying to defy you is kind of hazardous to our health."

The man surrendered as breezily as when he first walked up to Rika.

"But we still have a few things we absolutely *have* to do, mm-kay? I can take these two with me, yeah?"

"Wh-whoa!" protested Rika. He was obviously referring to Ashiya and Nord, Emi's father.

"I'm pretty sure I couldn't beat you even if I threw all my muscle into it, but...you know, if you aren't willing to give me that much, I'm not gonna have much choice apart from giving it the ol' college try."

"Even if all of you die?"

The man readily nodded at the woman's not-so-veiled threat. "I'd be dead anyway if I let a golden opportunity like this fall through my fingers."

"Stop all this nonsense!" Rika shouted, the tanned woman helping her recover from the initial shock. "Where're you taking Ashiya and Emi's dad?!"

"Didn't I just tell you, girl?" the strange man said, giving Rika a look. "I'm not taking them. They're just going back to where they used to be. And I'm assuming, if I'm judging you right, that you ain't gonna try to get in the way of that, mm-kay?"

"Hey, can...can you help them?" Rika asked. "I need you to help both of them!"

It was do-or-die time. This woman was the only person left to turn to. But as far as the other two were concerned, Rika was no longer a necessary part of the conversation.

"I think you probably already know this, but the older guy's on *this* side of things. So's the demon. They aren't part of Earth, so... fine by me."

This agreement from the ponytailed woman was nothing like what Rika had hoped for. An overwhelming presence loomed in her mind, enough to make the very rain around her seem to evaporate.

"I'm not allowed to interfere with anything like that, so go right ahead. Just stop screwing around over here, got it?"

"Got it. Thank youuuu!"

"No! No, come on! Please!"

At the man's signal, the knights once again picked Ashiya and Nord off the ground, along with the man previously smashed against the outer wall. All Rika could do was watch.

"Hey, what's your name?" asked the tanned woman.

"...Gabriel. The archangel Gabriel, although I'm kinda ashamed to say it lately."

"Yeah, I'll bet."

This crazy gang of armed soldiers was kidnapping two men, and she was just standing there in the rain, smiling like she enjoyed it.

"All right. So, Gabe—"

"You're giving me a nickname already?" the man called Gabriel moaned.

"You probably know this, too, but...I know I said *I* won't get in the way, but I can't guarantee that certain *other* people won't."

"Sure, sure. We can handle that. I promise we won't bother you anymore."

"We'll see about that. That's kinda the top two lies a man tells a woman, ain't it? 'I'm sorry,' and 'I won't do it again.'"

"Hah! Got me there. I've been around for a pretty long time, but compared to you, I'm still just a kid, aren't I?" The concept made Gabriel crack a smile. "I'd love to get your name, too, mm-kay?"

"...Nngh!"

Ashiya, carried by a knight behind Gabriel, chose that moment to twitch back to life. Rika immediately noticed.

"Ashiya!!"

"Oop, guess we went a little too easy on that human body of his," a disinterested Gabriel said.

"Wh-what on...? *Ngh!* Take your hands off me!"

Ashiya attempted to struggle, but his body wasn't up to the task. Several knights stepped in to hold him in place. He lifted his face upward in despair.

"*Grh*... M-Ms. Suzuki, are you all right...?"

Then he noticed the woman standing next to the muddied Rika. He recognized her. And the moment he did, his mind began racing. Gabriel visiting Sasazuka right when Emilia was away from Japan. The Efzahan knights from the Eastern Island. Himself and Nord, captured.

"Amane!!" he shouted. It was all clear now. He had been saved by Amane Ohguro, seasonal proprietor of the Ohguro-ya snack bar off the Choshi coast. She should've been occupied enough, running her little sanctuary for the dead over there, but now she was in Sasazuka for reasons Ashiya couldn't guess. He was at a loss as to why, but right now, she was all he had.

"Tell Maou I'll be waiting at the National Museum of Western Art!!"

"Hey, shut him up," Gabriel commanded.

A knight quickly placed a gauntlet over Ashiya's mouth—too late to keep him from getting across what he had to say. But it was a huge relief: Now, Maou ought to be able to handle the rest.

"You're Amane, huh?" Gabriel continued. "Hmm..."

"Yep. Amane Ohguro," she brightly chirped. "Not a bad guy, trust me. Oh, and roger that, Ashiya. That's all I gotta tell 'im?"

"Heh. Yeah, not a bad guy. Well, at least I didn't have to actually fight you, I guess. We sure lucked out this time, huh?"

"Oh, I wouldn't count my chickens quite yet. Those kids can be pretty tenacious."

"I know, mm-kay? I'm just not so sure that last ray of hope he's got is gonna come through this time. After all..." He turned up to the sky. "He's dealing with a guy that rules over everything 'red' in our world. With an iron fist, so to speak. I ain't too sure the Devil King can handle that right now."

"Everything 'red,' hmm?" Amane shrugged. "I don't remember hearing he can do that, but whatever. That's all your business, anyway, not mine. So, hey, are you leaving or what?"

"Wait... Wait a second!" Rika shouted.

"You got it, miss. Say hi to his boss for me, all right? I'd love to have him over sometime, actually."

And with that, they all disappeared. Before Rika's eyes, the dozens of men flicked out of existence like a TV screen, taking Ashiya and Nord with them.

"No...way..." Rika whispered, still on her knees in a puddle. And then:

"...*Oop.*"

She fell and fainted, finally overtaken by her fear and confusion. Amane gently held up her body, deftly carrying her piggyback as she looked around the area.

"Oh, brother... The Sephirots over on their world must be in a huge tizzy right now."

Adjusting Rika's position on her back, the ever-serene Amane walked up the Villa Rosa Sasazuka stairway. Room 201 was luckily unlocked—Rika and Ashiya must've forgotten to lock it as they ran from Gabriel.

"Sorry for barging in. This girl's gonna get a cold if I don't put some new clothes on her."

After stepping in, Amane placed Rika on the wooden floor in the kitchen area as she started looking for a towel. "Wow," she said as she marveled at the neatly folded pile of laundry. "He runs a tight ship... Hmm?"

As she plucked out two towels for herself and Rika, she noticed a sheaf of papers next to the laundry, something like a handwritten map written on the top sheet. She picked it up, toweling off her hair as she gave it a glance.

"Hmmm... So *that's* how it is. Ah, but I gotta change this girl's clothes first," Amane said as she began to remove Rika's ruined clothing. "You better not pick *this* exact moment to walk in, Maou."

Despite all the chaos that had just taken place, Amane sounded like this was an incredibly fun experience for her.

⁂

"Maaaaan, I've got a really bad feeling about this."

The half-demon Maou gave his sword a couple of test swings to see how it felt. It was light in his hand.

"This ain't demon force, is it? Something tells me the rebound from turning into this is gonna be a *total* bitch. Hopefully not, but I dunno..."

Maou might have been uneasy about his newfound powers, but despite his whining, he had just made five Heavenly Regiment soldiers eat dirt in a matter of seconds.

These soldiers wielded nowhere near the force of the archangel they served, but Camael's men were still massively more powerful and better trained than Gabriel's. Suzuno probably could have handled them, actually, if she didn't have to hold Chiho at the same time, but it was easy for Maou to imagine the difficulty she faced anyway.

It all happened in the blink of an eye, really. Every time Maou made a move, the roof of the building shuddered as a lightning-fast storm raged over it, the wind and sound barely keeping up. The Regiment soldiers fell like flies, as if the noise itself had stunned them. No one could even follow the action.

"Ooh... If it wasn't for Urushihara's spell, you'd be breaking a lot of windows right now..."

The sight was majestic enough for a rueful Chiho, her spirits now fully rallied, to get teary eyed as she watched.

Camael was still apparently satisfied with watching events from above, but all Libicocco could do was watch as the Regiment accompanying him was utterly routed.

"They aren't...dead, are they?" Chiho asked.

"I don't care."

Their shining red armor was all but flattened, shattered like a cookie someone had stepped on.

"You, Malebranche."

"...Yes."

Maou didn't bother looking at Libicocco. He didn't have to. His voice, along with what the demon had just witnessed, was enough to make him fall to his knees and grovel. He was not the Libicocco of the past. His head was to the ground, and he no longer tried to staunch the blood coming out of his stump.

"You better not ask me who I am by now, all right? 'Cause I am *not* in a good mood. I know you're kinda stuck between a rock and a hard place, but like I give a crap about that. You move even an inch, and I make you pay for it."

"...My liege."

Even if it wasn't demonic in nature, the force projected by the Devil King right now told Libicocco he had no choice but to yield.

"Right." Maou nodded as he lightly kicked off the ground and leaped over to Urushihara.

"...I'm...cuttin' it pretty close this time, dude..."

He was still on the roof, still unable to move so much as a finger, but not too weak to keep himself from carping at Maou.

"Yeah, well, hang in there. I'll take you to the hospital once it's all over."

"...Nice of you. That ain't too common."

"I didn't think that *he*"—Maou pointed at the figure in red high above them, still not moved to take action—"was dumb enough to go shootin' for your lazy ass first. You kept Chi and Suzuno safe, didn't you? Pretty good job."

"...I'm not...gonna give you anything...for that compliment..."

"Can you act appreciative for a single moment of your life, man? *I'm* the one dishing out favors right now."

If this was your normal, everyday demonic transformation, now would be the time when Maou would lend him some demonic force to heal him. But there was nothing demonic, nor holy, about what coursed through Maou now.

He turned his eyes to Camael.

"And you up there. What is this, like, the *n*th time you guys have messed around with me in Japan?"

He had to have heard the taunt, but Camael didn't move an inch.

"Not that I mind if you feel like meddling with us, but didn't your mom ever tell you not to be a bother to other people, no matter what?"

It was patently ridiculous, a demon lecturing an archangel on morals. But it was clear that a lot of angels up there had been violating the rule quite a bit lately.

"Whether you're scouting other people or transferring stuff here or there, people in this country say hello to each other first. They say 'please' and 'thank you.' They pay money for it. Sometimes they even sue each other. What they don't do is something as barbaric as start ripping the place apart the moment they show up."

"...Devil King," Camael finally said, his voice low and gravelly. "Satan."

"Yeah?"

"Devil King... Devil King Satan."

"Wh-what?"

With Libicocco yielding to him, the rain and wind had died down quite a bit. That was how Maou could notice that the trident spear in Camael's hand was rattling loudly in his gloved fingers.

"Devil...King...Overlord... Satan, Satan... Satan!"

"Wh-what're you doing? You're acting all weird."

Camael's voice ratcheted upward as he repeated the name, like a fuse burning toward some explosive end.

"Yet again, a demon by that name must get in my way?!"

"Wh-what? *You're* the ones always getting in *my* way!"

"Satan! Satan!!"

"Yahh!"

It came at a speed easily the equal of Maou's when he defeated the Regiment. The tips of Camael's trident glinted for just a moment—and the next, the spear was hurtling downward, ready to skewer him.

"Gnh!"

"Nrrgh!"

With blazing speed of his own, Maou reacted quickly enough to deflect the spear with his sword...

"Hyah!"

...and whirled around on the spot, throwing the sword toward Camael's armored chest.

Even as off balance as he was after the attack, the angel quickly took action. He swung his spear downward, hoping to absorb the force of the incoming blade. But the sword, which had crushed Regiment armor and cut off Libicocco's arm before he even realized what happened, was far keener than either of them even imagined.

"Eh?"

"Ngh?!"

Maou thought it was blocked. Camael must have thought so, too. But there was just a slight moment of resistance, when their weapons met—and then Maou realized he had made a clean follow-through.

"Ergh!"

Camael's muffled groan struck Maou's ears. Maou, for his part, was dumbfounded. Not only did the sword neatly lop off the top of the trident halfway down the handle, it then went on to slash right through the crimson armor like it was made of construction paper. It didn't make contact with skin below, it seemed—but not even Camael, who had reared back an instant after his weapon was cut in two, could believe the blade touched him.

Thoughts of battles fought long ago flashed in Maou's mind. Despite the overwhelming force now at his fingertips, he couldn't help but smile.

"...Man, I never had a chance against her, huh?"

His guard remained up, sword readied in front of him, as he kept a watchful eye on Camael's next move. Camael threw the hilt of his now-useless weapon aside, ran a hand across the newly-formed gash in his armor, and began to mutter.

"Satan... Satan, Satan...?"

"Uh?"

Maou could tell that his breathing was gradually becoming more labored.

"Sataaaann!!"

"What, what? You're freaking me out—whoa, whoa, whoa!"

He had thought Camael has lost his wits for a moment, but suddenly, the archangel took the remainder of the spear—the part with the pointy bits—and lunged forward.

"Satan!!"

The points of the spear were close to him now, close enough

that Maou could see the eyes behind the iron helmet—but he still blocked them easily. It wasn't that he didn't expect this surprise attack, but Camael's bizarre, and terrifying, behavior was starting to unnerve him.

"Gehh!"

Then things got even worse.

"Wh-whoa, are… What the hell?!"

The blade of Maou's sword, the one he used to defect the spear, was starting to eat between two of the trident's prongs with its eerily sharp blade. This made it physically clear just how fine a weapon it was, but it was exactly what Maou didn't want right now. If he cut through the space between the prongs, there wouldn't be anything there to keep the rest of the weapon from stabbing straight through him.

"G-geez!" Maou shouted in a panic. "This is too much of a good thing, man! Acieth, disengage!"

"Okay, Maou!"

Two things then happened at once. The sword in Maou's hand instantly dissolved into a swarm of light particles, which then gathered to a point below the two fighters. It created a human form, fusing upon itself at lightspeed to create a person. A girl, named Acieth Alla—the child of a Yesod fragment, just like Alas Ramus. And just as the now-freed trident was about to penetrate Maou's skin, Acieth's willowy fist punched right through the middle of it.

"Nngh!"

The dull thud that accompanied the onrush of force, something her arm never should have been capable of, made Camael's weapon go flying upward. He lost his balance on the rebound, leaving his torso wide open.

"Yahh!!"

It was greeted by a flying elbow from her wispy frame.

"Mngh!!"

Considering the size difference, the strike should have resulted in nothing but a broken elbow for Acieth. Instead, it sent cracks running across the midsection of Camael's armor like it was made of glass and sent his body somersaulting through the air before it crashed into the roof.

"Maou! What happened?!"

She was surprised to find Maou lying on the roof next to Camael's crumpled form.

"I lost my balance while I tried to dodge the spear, okay?!" Maou protested as he picked himself up.

"Maybe practice limbo dancing more, yes?"

"Devil Kings don't practice limbo dancing at all, lady!"

"...Dude, treat this seriously..."

Nobody heeded the words of Urushihara, still lying near the edge.

"I *am* serious!" Acieth replied. "Time to fight more! These guys, they are more enemy to me than Maou!"

Acieth's body, far more powerful (it turned out) than it looked, wriggled in the air as she struck what she presumably thought was a menacing fighting pose.

"Well, whatever you want, as long as you're helping us..."

Maou brought a finger to his forehead. This was Alas Ramus against Gabriel all over again. Acieth didn't evoke much confidence with her semifluent Japanese, but the hostility she bore for Camael sure seemed like the real thing to him. She wouldn't be expending all this strength on him otherwise. But what about Erone? He seemed to have no ill will toward Farfarello and the other demons at all. Was it just a matter of differing personalities?

"I wouldn't think so, no..."

"Ugh..."

"Yeah, I didn't think that'd be enough to do him in," Maou said as the sight of Camael struggling to his feet distracted him.

"Sataaann!!"

"Oh, great, me again? What's your problem with me, anyway?"

Maou was 100 percent sure they had never met before. He'd never seen any angels at all, in fact, until he went to Japan.

"I mean, I don't really wanna sic Acieth on you if I don't even know what you're angry about..."

"Oh, I am okay with it!"

"Chill out a sec, all right?" Maou said, attempting to calm her for a moment so that he could think in peace.

"...Yeah, just chill out, mm-kay? You too, Camael."

Maou and Acieth both reared back, creating distance from the voice that suddenly popped up.

"Ga—"

"Gabriel!!" Acieth shouted before Maou could finish, voice tinged with even more hatred than what she lodged at Camael.

"Whoa, wait—what?!" Gabriel exclaimed, rather surprised himself as he gaped at her.

"W-wait, Acieth!"

Maou had to quickly step in to keep the girl from leaping for Gabriel's jugular right then and there.

"What, Maou? Lemme do it!"

"Wait, wait!" he said, grabbing her arm as he watched Gabriel. "We finally got someone I can actually talk to here! Don't go killing him before I can at least do that!"

He didn't expect much from this new visitor—more of the meandering, misleading nonsense that Gabriel had given him last time—but at least he was more capable of coherent speech than Camael or Libicocco.

"Acieth...?"

Gabriel, meanwhile, sighed at the sight of the silver-haired girl who was ready to kill him at first sight.

"My, my, my. All these unplanned events, one after the other..."

"You pulling more of this behind-the-scenes crap again?" Maou asked, more exasperated than surprised by now. Whenever there was strife in his life, Gabriel always seemed to be part of it.

"Well, yeah, uh... Or I s'pose you could say that it wasn't so behind-the-scenes, mm-kay? Kinda different now, though. If that makes me a rat, then gimme some cheese to gnaw on, huh?"

He shrugged in self-depreciating fashion.

"I'm going home, Camael. If we keep trying to be greedy like this, it's gonna bite us in the ass, that much I'm pretty sure of. This latent force is enough of a pain in the butt, but *now* we got someone waaaaaay rougher getting into the mix."

Camael's stomach heaved up and down.

"Boy, someone's in a real tizzy, huh?"

"I think something's wrong with him, Gabriel."

Maou couldn't help but butt in at the sight. Gabriel's suggestion to retreat seemed to not register with Camael at all. He simply kept breathing, loudly and heavily.

"Yeah. Guess he can't keep cool when Devil King Satan's around."

"Uh, I don't think we have a beef with each other, do we? We haven't even met."

"Hey, don't bitch at me, mm-kay? Bitch at your mom 'n' dad for naming you Satan in the first place. Maybe things'd be different if you were the Devil King Jimmy or something, but—"

"What's so bad about Jimmy? You got a problem with the Jimmys of the world?"

"Yeah, sure, tell 'em all I said sorry for me. Come on, Camael, let's go. We can't flex our full muscle in this world anyway, and neither can they. There's some seriously bad hombres gettin' involved, mm-kay?"

"Wait, you're going?" Maou snarled. They seemed ready to take off, but he wasn't ready to let them fly the coop quite yet. "No explanation or apology or anything?"

"Yeah, um... Let's just say that, uh, what I saw freaked me out so much that I want outta here ASAP, yeah?"

"What?"

"Um... Hey, you. The biggest bum in the world."

Gabriel stepped toward the prone Urushihara, chiding him. Maybe he was still sore about how he treated him earlier.

"You still got that business card I gave you, right?"

"*Business* card?" Maou glared at Gabriel, wondering what archangels needed something like that for.

"...It's at the bottom of one of my drawers. Covered in dust."

"Well, take better care of it than *that,* all right? Those things don't exactly grow on trees, y'know! That really hurts my feelings!" Gabriel nodded perfunctorily, a twinge of sadness to his voice. "Anyway, that bum has my phone number, so gimme a call later, mm-kay? Oh, and here's a little...uh, something for your trouble?"

He clapped his hands once. Maou and Acieth steeled themselves for the worst, but instead a soft light extended out from the roof to cover the entire school grounds, before vanishing in the blink of an eye.

"I kept all the storm damage intact 'cause it'd be too weird otherwise, but with *that*, nobody in this school has any memory of the past hour or so. So can we call ourselves even for now?"

"..."

Maou paused. He found himself looking at his feet, then at Chiho and Suzuno behind him.

"For now...? You planning a rematch later on?"

"Hey, if you're up for it."

"I'd prefer not to, man."

"Even if I told you that we're in possession of Emilia the Hero's body?"

"......!"

To some extent, he was expecting Gabriel to say that. Considering how much the angels preferred to keep their diabolical plans under wraps and unnoticed, he knew they'd risk a flashy, destructive strike on Japan for one reason, and one reason only—because the Hero Emilia, the greatest current threat to their way of life, was gone. Hearing it from Gabriel's mouth, though, made every muscle on Maou's face tense up.

"Ooh, that's a funny face you're making! Not exactly the kinda thing I'd expect the King of All Demons to make, mm-kay?"

Gabriel smiled, the sheer joy behind it something that Maou had never seen from him before.

"Well, see you later, Devil King...or should I say, the latest disaster we have to deal with?"

*

And so Gabriel went "home"—but not after trashing Sasahata North High; taking Camael, the Regiment, and Libicocco with him; and leaving a bombshell revelation in his wake. "Home," in this case, was much more likely Ente Isla than the heavenly realm.

"Goddammit," spat Maou as he looked at the now-calmer sky. It was almost two in the afternoon. He should have been on a train back home by now, all smiles after acing his road test. "Where the hell am I gonna get the money for a third exam?"

But as he shook an angry fist at the skies above, Maou realized something. His body was back to its human self—back to good ol' Sadao Maou. Surprised, he turned to Acieth, who was still yelling something toward the area Gabriel disappeared into.

"...This makes zero sense."

Maou set off. Getting Suzuno and Urushihara patched up came first.

"You all right, Chi?"

"Ah..." Chiho looked down at herself. Her uniform, as well as her face and hands, were stained with muddy red blood. It was a sight to behold.

"I'm...fine?"

She nodded, and then tears began to well in her eyes.

"This is...all...Suzuno's blood. She tried to protect me..."

"...She did?"

"Gnhh..."

The prone Suzuno groaned out loud. She sounded like she was ready to faint.

"I-I'll go fetch my 5-Holy Energy β bottle from my classroom! Suzuno needs some right now!"

"Wait a sec, Chi!" Maou shouted. "You can't go back lookin' like that!"

Chiho being witnessed by other students in her current bloodied state would, at the very least, have an impact on her social life.

"Let's go back to my apartment for now. Acieth?"

"Don't run, monster! Come back here now! We will fight this fair and square, chicken!"

"Acieth!"

"I hate you! All stupid angels! Next time, it will be the last time! You wait and see, I tell you! You assholes!"

"Acieth!!"

It took a lot of lung power to wrest Acieth's attention away from her apparent nemesis. He sighed, a sense of fatigue suddenly overcoming him.

"Can you take all of us here over to my apartment?"

"One, two, three… Uh-huh! No prob!"

Maou wondered whether she really needed to count them or not.

"Who…is this girl, Maou?" Chiho asked.

"Hold that thought, Chi. We gotta get Suzuno and Urushihara home first. You're coming with us, too—we can talk then. We've gotta discuss Emi, too."

"Oh…!"

The reminder startled Chiho. She must have heard Gabriel as well as Maou did.

"So… Wait, Maou, are you gonna go and res—"

"We'll talk about that, too, okay? Let's go. Acieth!"

"Okay!" Acieth gave a pointless thumbs-up and clapped her hands. "Hop on!"

"Ah!"

"Oof…"

"Ngh!"

Chiho, Suzuno, and Urushihara all floated in the air, Maou and Acieth joining them a moment later.

"Take it slow, okay? I don't want anyone to notice us."

"Bossy, bossy, bossy! I will try. I gave my body to you long time, after all."

"…Please don't phrase it like that."

Maou, seeing that Chiho was too busy tending to Suzuno behind him to notice the statement, felt a sudden sense of relief. Acieth wasn't wrong, exactly, but that statement alone would be enough for Emi to slice Maou in half lengthwise if she was around.

"Nah-ha-ha! You look funny. Okay, here we go!"

With that signal, the five of them gently glided through the light drizzle that now fell over the school.

"We'll be there soon, all right?" Chiho said, using a handkerchief to keep Suzuno's and Urushihara's faces dry along the way. "Hang in there. We've got some 5-Holy Energy β in your room, Suzuno."

"Some" didn't describe it. There was virtually a lifetime supply of holy magic now stored in her apartment. That would be enough to help revive the two of them, and it seemed safe to assume that no further threat to their lives was forthcoming.

Maou kept an eye on them as he thought through his leads. It was vital for him, once he got back home, to extract all the information he could from Acieth and Nord and get a full grip on their current situation. But already he had the suspicion that no matter what the picture looked like, his plan of action looked the same in the end.

"Back to...*that* world, huh?"

Back to Ente Isla, the Land of the Holy Cross, the human world he was once a hairbreadth away from conquering.

"Too bad we wound up half-assing it so much."

It was an expression of regret that Maou wouldn't have even dared let Ashiya hear, muttered to no one in particular as they floated above the Shuto Expressway traffic. As a conqueror of mankind, as the supreme leader of demondom, he had failed to fulfill his full duties as Devil King. Now he was slumming it here in Japan, living day to day with seemingly not a care in the world. Was that really all right? The doubt had taken up permanent residence in his mind.

He wanted to learn everything he had access to in this world, and then he wanted to bring it back to the demon realms. That much was the truth. But before he could pursue that dream, he felt, there were certain things he had to do.

"I gotta do something about my shifts before anything else... Wasn't exactly expecting to fail twice, so I didn't schedule any more days off this month... Hope I can find someone to cover a shift for me..."

That was another concern of his, yes. Flying over Hatagaya Station must have made Maou's mind jump the track a bit. He shook it off.

"But now...? I can't do a thing by myself anymore."

He needed Chiho, and Suzuno, and Urushihara, and—

"I need all of their strength."

⁂

"Oh, they're back. Heeeyyy!"

A familiar voice greeted them from below. Maou and Chiho looked down to find someone waving at them outside the Devil's Castle front door. They were shocked.

"Amane?!"

"Huh?"

It was Amane Ohguro, their summer-job boss from Choshi. She was the niece of Miki Shiba, the corpulent landlord at Villa Rosa Sasazuka, so it wasn't too strange that she knew Maou's address. But he still remembered what she'd pulled off above the waters of Choshi, and the bizarre and undoubtedly superhuman way she'd disappeared from their lives.

"Oh, great, another lead to pursue," Maou mumbled to himself. It took only a few more moments for him to realize that it was far more than that.

"*...Guh.*"

Urushihara slipped down onto the floor of the interior hallway upon losing Maou's support. Neither Maou nor Chiho (currently keeping Suzuno upright), had any ability to help him now. That was because both Ashiya and Nord were gone from Devil's Castle—and in its place was a scraped-up Rika Suzuki, sleeping like the dead and wearing clothes taken from Maou's closet.

"Um... Amane?" he asked, voice shaking.

"Yep?"

"Where're Ashiya and the...older guy who was just here?"

"Kidnapped," Amane blurted as she quietly helped Urushihara up. "Right in front of me, too."

"K-kidnapped?!" Chiho shouted, too surprised to do anything but parrot the word back at her. "Ashiya?!"

"All I was capable of doing," Amane calmly replied, "was keeping this woman safe." She pointed at the recumbent Rika as she placed

Urushihara down a little ways from her. "It was them against this gang of armored knights and this lanky goofball named Gabriel."

""...!"" Neither Maou nor Chiho could hide their shock.

"I'm guessing you were expecting this?"

Yes and no. Certainly it made sense that Gabriel would want to seize one of Emi's relatives if he was still after the holy sword and Yesod fragments. But why Ashiya, too? It only served to confuse Maou even more—and Chiho, who hadn't heard about the events at the DMV yet.

Amane sized them up, then nodded. Rising quickly to her feet, she presented Maou with a sheaf of papers Ashiya had kept next to the laundry.

"What's this...?" he asked.

"It's written in some script I can't read. Looks like a map or something, but..."

"It's Centurient...in Ashiya's handwriting."

"Also," Amane interrupted, as she noticed Chiho peeking at the stack of papers, "don't you think you should be patching up Suzuno right now, Chiho? You look pretty soaked yourself, too. You're gonna die from the flu if you don't dry out."

"Oh! Right! Sorry, Suzuno, but I need to go into your room, okay?"

The color returned to Chiho's face as Suzuno groaned her approval. They both went into the still-unlocked apartment.

"Whoa! Wow, it's a complete mess in here... Uh, h-how about you just sit down here, Suzuno...?"

Maou listened to Chiho's startled reaction through the wall as he studied the papers. Slowly, the meaning behind them dawned on him.

"...This is a map of the Eastern Island. The cities, the road links, what areas the other islands have influence in, what the central mountain tribes fighting against Efzahan are up to... There's some top secret information in here, too. What was he doing with this...?"

Maou knew that Ashiya had taken to spending a lot of his time writing lately. *Is this the product of that?* But before he could figure out what his general had left this behind for...

"Also, Ashiya left me a message for you."

"A message?"

"Yeah," she slowly said. "To you. He said he'd be 'waiting at the National Museum of Western Art.' That's all. I don't know what it means."

"The National Museum… That's in Ueno. Ashiya went there on research trips a few times…"

The Tokyo neighborhood of Ueno was home to a number of large national museums. Maou recalled how they both paid numerous visits to most of them early on, exploring planet Earth's occult history in an effort to find a way back home.

"So that map's from your world?"

"Oh, um…"

Then Maou remembered his present situation. Amane was… unusual, no doubt about that. But how did she know from the first time they met in Choshi that he and Suzuno, for that matter, weren't from Earth? And that went for Miki Shiba, her aunt and their landlord, too, right?

Amane shook her head as Maou pondered over this. "I told you before, didn't I? I can't tell you anything if Aunt Mikitty hasn't already told you. That's how the rules work."

"Oof…" Maou groaned, discouraged at Amane's indifference to his plight. Then he heard Rika moan as she squirmed to life on the floor. He thought she had woken up, but instead she settled back down after a moment. It was a relief to Maou that she was sleeping at least, and not unconscious.

But then—

"Ashi…ya…"

"She's talking in her sleep?"

"…Help…Ashiya… Help me…"

"Yeahhh, it musta been pretty scary for her, I guess. She's just a normal woman, besides. I'm sure Ashiya and the other guy tried their best to protect her, but…"

That reminded Maou of another key point. Emi and Alas Ramus were on Ente Isla—and now, that almost certainly applied to Ashiya and Emi's father. They were all back where they used to be—but now, it was undeniably hostile territory to them. Whose job was it, then, to save them? What needed to be done?

How could he get back to Ente Isla?

He couldn't use his own powers. And he still didn't know what he was dealing with in Acieth. His Gate abilities were powered by demonic force, anyway; there was no guarantee he could build a stable one with any other sort of power source.

So who could open a Gate right now? Didn't Suzuno say it herself? That you could open one as long as you had the right amplifier?

And Ashiya was waiting at the National Museum of Western Art…

Maou looked up.

"A Gate… That's it! A Gate! Hey! Suzuno!"

Leaping out of Devil's Castle, Maou zoomed down the hall and banged on Suzuno's door.

"M-Maou, wait a…! Y-you can't come in right now!"

Maou ignored Chiho's pleas and opened the door wide.

"Oh…"

"Ah…"

"Maou!!"

The moment he stepped in, Maou's face ran right into a curtain with some kind of intricate pattern drawn on it.

"I *told* you, you can't come in!!" Chiho continued to admonish.

What Maou saw in the dimly lit room before this curtain blinded him was Chiho providing Suzuno an energy drink as she took a wet towel to her wounds, and:

"M…Maou…youuuuuu…"

And Suzuno, whose kimono was stripped down to her waist as Chiho tended to the gash on her shoulder.

"Oh, uh… S-sorry! I'm sorry, but listen to me! This is really impor—*ow*!"

"Just get *out* of here, Maou!!"

"Gahh!"

From the other side of the curtain, something rather blunt hit Maou in the forehead with enough force to bend him backward. He toppled over, but came back up to his feet, head still caught in the curtain. He had to get this across to her, now.

"Maou, you're really starting to make me angry, okay?!"

"You…*truly* wish to die…do you not? *Ngh…*"

Even in her current state, the murderous intent was clear in Suzuno's muffled words.

"Hey! Oh, Maou! We are one, now, heart and soul! And now you peek at the naked ladies?!"

Even through the curtain, Maou could tell that Acieth's timely entry into the room made that murderous rage grow even hotter.

"I better call the police… Hey, Urushihara, is there a phone in here?"

"Dude, I'm… I'm a lot more hurt than I look, so…"

Listening to the sad exchange between Amane and Urushihara next door made Maou feel like he was getting completely shoehorned out of the picture. He left the room—or Acieth dragged him out, more like—and spoke to Suzuno through the closed door. The first thing he spotted as he lifted the curtain from his head was the giant hardback Japanese dictionary that Chiho apparently threw at him.

"H-hey, Suzuno!"

"…Whaaaaat?"

It was weird. She sounded so weak and frail, but the tone of it still made Maou's hair stand on end.

"Y-you can beat me up all you want later, so just listen for a sec, okay?"

"Ooh, you like, Maou?"

"Shut *up*, Acieth! Suzuno, listen! You said we could open a Gate if we had the right amplifier, yeah?!"

"…I did," came the gravelly reply.

Maou's eyes lit up. "I think we got one! There's an amplifier I think you can use at the National Museum of Western Art in Ueno!"

"…In Ueno? A holy-magic amplifier?"

Chiho seemed not to understand Maou's words. Suzuno, on the other hand, furrowed her brows.

"L-let me just say… *Ngh…*"

"Suzuno!"

"N-no... I am fine. Devil King, the 'Stairs of Heaven' have been the subject of people's faith for generations. They were carved out of the very earth following oral traditions and those of our scriptures. They are the largest of amplifiers, providing a meaningful contribution to the very concept of holy magic. I do not wish to discount my adoptive home for the time being, but I sincerely doubt any object in Japan would be the object of such a high level of faith and power—to say nothing of an object so close by..."

"There *is*, all right? There is! And we don't even have to pay to get in! It's the *Gates of Hell*!"

"The gates of...hell?" Chiho and Suzuno looked at each other. Maou was starting to sound more like the Devil King again, although they could tell how much he emphasized the free-entry aspect of it.

"Have you ever seen it before, Chi?" Maou confidently asked. "That really big bronze sculpture outside the front entrance of the National Museum of Western Art in Ueno?"

Chiho searched her memory as she wrung out her towel.

"...I think I might've, during a school field trip or something. Like, isn't *The Thinker* posing above the gates or something?"

"Yeah, that!" Maou eagerly replied.

The piece depicted a scene from "The Inferno," the opening chapter of the *Divine Comedy*, in which Dante is guided by an ancient poet through the various circles of Hell. It is depicted not as a land of anguish where the dead pay for living a sinful life, but as a world of holiness, created by God as part of His grand scheme. *The Gates of Hell* was crafted by Auguste Rodin, hailed as the father of modern sculpture; the one at the National Museum was one of seven bronze casts that exist throughout the world, continually absorbing the story of mankind's thoughts, faiths, and histories as they accumulated over time.

"It's the entrance to hell as it was described in the *Divine Comedy*. That's exactly what it depicts!"

"So, so..."

"It might...be worth trying, yes."

"Yeah, totally! I know we can open a Gate with that! So heal up already, man! You too, Urushihara!"

Maou wrested the curtain from his head and spiked it on the floor to emphasize the point.

"Ashiya, Nord, Alas Ramus...and Emi, too! We're gonna save 'em all!"

EXTRA CHAPTER
THE HERO HAS A CRY

Today marked day fourteen since Emi was taken to the prison cell disguised as a luxury retreat. Watching the vast ocean expand out through her windowside view, she let out a light sigh.

She hadn't thought there was anything dangerous about it, so why did it have to turn out like this?

"Mommy!"

"...Alas Ramus, if you keep playing up there, you're gonna fall off the bed again."

The bed was of exquisite make, and Alas Ramus was currently using it as a trampoline.

They had not been bound or chained to a dungeon wall. Nothing of the sort. And no physical harm had been done to either of them. And the window was a simple glass affair—window glass itself being a rare, costly commodity in this world. She didn't need the Better Half to smash it; throwing the writing desk that occupied a corner of the room at it would do the trick well enough. The key to the room was in Emi's possession.

"...I bet everybody's worried by now."

The room overlooked Phaigan, a military port on the far northwestern edge of the Eastern Island. It was the site of a large naval base that also saw use as a commercial port, and the area behind the base was occupied by a fairly decent-sized city. Once a humble fishing village, it was now the nearest port to Skycastle, the capital of Efzahan, steadily growing over the years. It was also the birthplace of the ancestors of the Azure Emperor, Efzahan's supreme leader.

Emi had visited here once during her quest to slay the Devil King. She still had a decent lay of the land. It was the last of the islands to be freed from its Great Demon General, and that—combined with the authoritarian regime that preceded demon rule—made it seem like a rather dull, dreary city, especially compared to the vast settlements on the Western Island and the lively, multiethnic towns of the Northern Island.

From her vantage point, it seemed like the city had grown even gloomier than before, although Emi's current mood was no doubt coloring that impression.

"Chiho… Bell… Sorry I broke my promise."

It was a statement Emi had whispered into the air multiple times over the past two weeks.

How great it would have felt to tell them directly. She knew the holy force that streamed into her from the moment she returned to Ente Isla was several orders of magnitude more than what she had in Japan. She could probably send an Idea Link, for example, without requiring an amplifier like Chiho did.

But…

"…"

"Loyal and brave fighters of Efzahan!"

Emi winced as she placed her hands over her ears. Alas Ramus, hearing the same sound, grimaced.

"We will now announce the results of the sea battle fought around the offshore islands to the northwest…"

It was, Emi presumed, a regular broadcast sent to pump up morale around Phaigan whenever a skirmish involving the port took place. The broadcast equipment of Earth didn't exist here, of course, but the involvement of an amplifier—for holy force, not for electricity—was one similarity.

They must have had a large facility for housing this force, and she guessed that the port was equipped with sonar equipment for monitoring holy-power usage within the military base. If she sent an Idea Link to another world with no amplifier, that might cost her whatever freedom she had left right now. She didn't mind that, but the image of Alas Ramus being thrown into some dank, underground dungeon kept her from acting.

And even before considering that, there was also the fact that Emi's mobile phone had been confiscated. That restricted her options even further. She gritted her teeth, thinking about the events that bought her here to Phaigan. The people of this land, at least, had no reason to take her smartphone away—it clearly wasn't a weapon. Emi was not a sorceress by trade—without that phone serving as an amplifier, she wasn't too confident that she could accurately send an Idea Link to a specific person in Japan.

Although, there was one person.

"Well… I hope Rika's okay…"

Emi recalled the face of the only friend in Japan she was able to make contact with.

Even if she didn't have anything in her possession, Chiho could send a targeted Idea Link to someone nearby if she knew the target's phone number. Remembering this, Emi pictured Rika's number in her mind—the only number she had memorized besides her own—and that let her make a pinpoint connection. She had it down cold because, since she didn't know how her smartphone's contact list worked at first, she looked up the number from the workplace directory and typed it in manually each time.

In order to avoid holy-force detection, she made sure to send the Link only when a military broadcast was taking place. These broadcasts were considerably detailed, covering not only battle results but also seaside weather forecasts and what the nobility were doing over in the capital. They tended to go on for a while, which gave her a decent amount of leeway. But…

"…Rika…"

Emi regretted contacting her now. Rika knew nothing about Emi and the people around her. She had thought that if she contacted Rika on a different day from the last time she spoke to Maou, that would lead Maou or Suzuno to realize something was up once Rika brought it up with them. It wasn't until the second call, however, that she realized doing this exposed Rika to the risk of getting wrapped up in Ente Islan events. If that put her in danger... Emi couldn't even imagine how she could apologize for it.

"This is what I get for living a lie all this time, I guess..."

"Mommy, you okay?"

Now Alas Ramus was at her feet, giving her a worried look.

"Alas Ramus?"

"Yah?"

"...I want you to never lie to your friends, all right? Ever."

"Lie?"

Alas Ramus, apparently, was still too young to understand the concept. She gave Emi a questioning look, but Emi remained silent, eyes turned back toward the swells on the sea.

"...What would they even do, though? Like, even *if* Rika contacted them?"

Urushihara wouldn't give a crap. Ashiya would probably do a jig right on the spot. And maybe Maou would be a little unnerved—he *did* care about Alas Ramus—but he couldn't care less about Emi. And part of her didn't want him to.

"No way..."

So what was she expecting, then, when she gave Rika an Idea Link?

"...Ahh!"

Emi covered her face with her hands, holding them tight as she gritted her teeth. She had to, or else the unbelievable reality she just thought of was going to physically pin her to the ground.

You have to be kidding. That's impossible.

"I don't want them to...help me..."

How could she live with herself if the Devil King flew in to the rescue? Whenever he helped her in the past, there was always an ulterior motive, another goal that Maou was hoping to achieve for himself.

"Mommy, you're okay."

"Alas Ramus..."

"Daddy's coming."

"……"

She had yet to explain the current situation to the child. She doubted she'd understand, and if anything, she seemed to be enjoying this little coastal vacation. But Alas Ramus still managed to expertly jab her "mommy" right where she was weakest.

"…You know what, Alas Ramus? Daddy's…Daddy's busy with work. Mommy's gonna have to handle things for herself for a while, all right? She's a Hero, after all."

"Hero?"

"Yeah, so…"

"Do you have to?"

Another bout of silence. Children could be so cruel sometimes.

Emi tried to flee the innocent question. A question from the girl who loved her as a mother.

"Well… I guess I do, yeah. But if someone does show up, it'd be a lot better to have Suzuno or Emeralda, I think."

"I wanna see Suzu-Sis! An' Chi-Sis, too! An' Al-cell 'n' Looshifer!"

"Um…yeah. Yeah, I bet you do."

"*Waph!*"

Emi picked Alas Ramus up and held her tight—tight enough to make the child squirm a little. The salty air of the Ente Isla seaside, the land she had wanted to return to so badly, now strained her heart to its breaking point.

A knock sounded on the door. Emi hurriedly placed Alas Ramus back on the floor. "One second!" she said as she fused the girl back into her own body. She didn't want Alas to see how she interacted with the person on the other side—the cold, dark sneer, so unbecoming of a Hero.

She sighed, wiped the corners of her eyes, and then glared at the door, as if firing bullets through it.

"All right, come in."

"Pardon me."

It was a voice from way back. One that had a calming effect on her, long ago. Now, it sounded nothing less than hateful.

"…What do you want, Olba?"

It was Olba Meiyer, one of the six Bishops of the Church and a central part of Emi's quest to rid the world of the demon scourge. Maou in demon form defeated him when he used Urushihara to attack Sasazuka, but—as she learned from the demon Camio in Choshi—he somehow escaped custody and made his way back to Ente Isla. Coming to Phaigan, however, and seeing him in the flesh once more, filled her with such a black, sinister sense of hatred. It surprised her, how much rage she could feel against someone she used to count on as a close confidant.

"I am here because I have something to give you. You don't have to be so angry at me. I will not be long."

"Anything you give me, you know I'm giving right back to the maid later on."

"Ha-ha-ha… Well, I suppose I understand your feelings, but I'm not so sure you can do that with this, exactly. It is, after all, one of the reasons why you came here in the first place."

The tonsure on his head still bore a scar from the battle in Sasazuka on it. It stuck out in Emi's eyes as Olba took out what appeared to be a plain hemp pouch from his Church robe.

"I wanted to prove to you that we are sticking to our promise. I have a sample to show you. Seeing the real thing, I presume, will help put your mind at ease slightly."

The pouch was resting in Olba's wrinkled palm. It appeared to have some weight to it. Emi noticed the string tying the opening shut, as well as the leaf someone had stuck into the side fabric. It made her open her eyes wide. Both the leaf and the string had been specially treated to serve as drying agents, meant to fend off moisture when storing crops long-term.

"It appears you already know what it is, inside here?"

Olba grinned as he brought his other hand to the string.

"Wait!" Emi shouted, eyes darting between the pouch and the view out the window. "If you open that here…!"

"I apologize, but handing it to you and having you do nothing with it would be rather pointless, wouldn't it?"

Before she could stop him, Olba had it open, pouring the contents into a water pitcher on the table in front of the door.

"Stop!"

But it was too late. The contents flowed in, floating for a moment in the salt-tinged water inside before taking in the moisture and falling to the bottom. Emi recognized them as wheat seeds, and a look of despair crossed her face as they settled down.

"Don't worry. As I said, this is just a sample. We've got quite an inventory to work with. Do you understand that we are keeping our promise now?"

Olba tossed the empty pouch near the pitcher.

"As I mentioned earlier, Emilia, if you are willing to listen to what you are told, I promise you that our 'hostages' will be well taken care of by our experts from the Western Island. But if you try to do anything strange, it will all end up like this."

He gestured toward the seeds.

"The stage is almost set. I hope you will rest yourself well for what is to come."

Then he left the room, not bothering to wait for the dumbfounded Emi's reply. By the time his footsteps were no longer audible, Emi was on her knees.

The wheat seeds were not from this land. The high salt content of the drinking water here, on this faraway island, rendered the seeds useless the moment they absorbed it. That was the great cause, the invisible manacles keeping her here and forcing her to do her mortal enemy's bidding.

"Mommy..."

The worried voice of Alas Ramus rang in her head. But Emi was no longer capable of responding.

This is how a Hero works? She was no Hero. She was just a powerless peon. Even after everything they had done to her, she still couldn't dare lift her sword.

"H...help...someone..."

The soft sound of falling tears was lost amid the ever-present waves of the sea, never reaching the ears of anyone besides Emi and Alas Ramus.

– To be continued –

THE AUTHOR, THE AFTERWORD, AND YOU!

Ever since I was young, I've always had kind of a thing for work vehicles. The impact they have on every aspect of Japanese manufacturing, logistics, and consumer activity—as well as the efforts of everyone who operate them in their work—is something I have to pay my respects to.

This sense of awe comes to mind whenever I see big construction trucks, or the assorted specialized vehicles you see running around airports. I get it even when I see regular trucks and haulers running around town. It's like a little tingle. The first time I had the chance to drive a pickup truck, I was struck at the incredible power stored within such a relatively compact car. Later, when I drove a Toyota HiAce van around, I was shocked at how it remained just as spry and handleable even when I helped my friend move and he packed it to the gills with stuff.

With that in mind, it's perhaps only natural that I've had a similar thing for the special scooters used by pizza places and the like, the ones with rear-mounted cargo containers. I love the three-wheeled one with roofs, in particular, simply because they look so completely different from normal motorcycles. *So* cool. Sadly, nobody in my social circle understands the attraction. Not yet, anyway.

When I was writing this volume, I gave more than half a thought to purchasing one of those tricycle scooters, figuring it'd come in handy and wouldn't cost as much as a car to maintain. I was wrong. Those things are built for maneuverability, and that comes at a cost—about three times your average scooter new. You could buy a cheap, low-powered used car with that kind of budget.

Another issue is that apparently I have a freakishly enormous head or something, because about the only helmet that fits me is an XXXL (64 cm or larger). That, combined with the insurance I'll have to take out for it, adds further to the cost. I'm probably gonna have to consider it for a while longer.

Still, owning a vehicle with an engine definitely allows you more range, not to mention versatility. It comes with a certain level of social responsibility, too (the obligation to be licensed, respect traffic laws, etc.), but it's hard to beat the way it can expand the world for you.

If you're reading this, that means that the current date is either April 10, 2013, or (more likely) some date after that. You might already be aware of this by the time you pick this book up, but April marks the broadcast launch of the *Devil Is a Part-Timer!* animated series. This means the world of *Devil* has expanded once again—from book, to manga, and now to anime. I think it'll be fun for viewers to discover new ways to interact with this world, and I also think giving people the chance to explore it in all these different ways makes it a better work overall.

Between Akio Hiiragi's manga version of *Devil*, Kurone Mishima's spinoff, *The Devil is a Part-Timer! High School!*, and the upcoming anime version directed by Naoto Hosoda, there are now so many different ways for all of us to enjoy the world of Sadao Maou and Emi Yusa. There really are. And as the main man behind all this, it couldn't make me happier.

And, with Volume 8 of the *Devil* novels, I think it's fair to say that the story is going in new and downright shocking directions. The world is expanding once again for readers, and this volume marks the kickoff. It's only going to be more frenetic in the next volume, and I hope you guys won't mind the wait too much.

But even though this volume launches a thrilling new story arc that crosses worlds and *may just change everything*, the characters that inhabit it are exactly as they've always been. The Devil King and the Hero are working hard to keep themselves afloat, because if you want to change, you have to take that first step. I imagine that's the credo all of them live by—the Devil King, the Hero, the teenage girl, the demons, the clerics, and the angels.

But no matter how noble the cause, it's still not nice to make reckless remarks in your work. Therefore, in closing, I would like to apologize on behalf of the tall, airheaded archangel in the story who personally offended every single man and woman named "Jimmy" or some variant thereof.

Here's hoping I'll see you in the next volume.

Farewell!

Congratulations on completing Vol. 8!
This is Akio Hiiragi, creator of the comic version running in *Dengeki Daioh* magazine.
The anime broadcast is just about to kick off! I can't wait to check it out—I'll be joining the ranks of all you other viewers!